Harriet Dark

ABOUT THE BOOK

Branwell Brontë, brother of the Brontë sisters, described to his friends a novel which he had written but which was not discovered among his papers after his death. Barbara Rees ingeniously has now reconstructed this novel.

She has written a brilliant gothic novel whose literary value is firmly based in Brontë tradition. Harriet Dark is a foundling who proves no easier to accommodate at the great Yorkshire home of Robert Ogilvy than was the foundling Heathcliff at Wuthering Heights. Harriet sets herself to avenge the loss of her beloved mother by allying herself to the devil. She thereby contrives the death of Nina Sanctuary, perhaps Branwell's answer to Blanche Ingram.

Barbara Rees is a formidable novelist in her own right. Apart from creating a brilliant reinterpretation of the Brontës, she has taken up and illuminated larger themes about the nature of womanhood and good and evil.

ABOUT THE AUTHOR

Barbara Rees has won a place of distinction amongst novelists today: "A smooth and adroit writer" (*New Yorker*), "a writer of high caliber and sophistication" (*Publishers Weekly*), "imaginative and honest" (*Library Journal*), "good writing" (*New York Times*). Her previous novels include *Try Another Country*, *Diminishing Circles*, *Prophet of the Wind*, *George and Anna* and recently for Gordon & Cremonesi, a volume on *The Victorian Lady*.

Harriet Dark
Branwell Brontë's Lost Novel

Barbara Rees

Gordon & Cremonesi

Designed by Heather Gordon
Set in 11 on 12 pt Palatino
by Input Typesetting Ltd.
Printed in Great Britain by litho at The Anchor Press Ltd
and bound by Wm Brendon & Son Ltd
both of Tiptree, Essex

British Library Cataloguing in Publication Data
Rees, Barbara
Harriet Dark.
I Title
823'.9'1F PR6068.E367H/ 78–40405

LCCN: 78–040405
ISBN: 0–86033–075–3

Gordon & Cremonesi Publishers
London and New York
New River House,
34 Seymour Road
London N8 0BE

FOR COLIN
the book of 1977

Chapter One

MY NAME is Harriet Dark. I came to live at Thirleby Hall in the North Riding of Yorkshire in the year 1829, when I was five years old—or six, or four. No one knows for certain, any more than is known the name I was born with. For Harriet Dark was the name I was given by my new owner, Mr Robert Bartholomew Ogilvy, who acquired me upon a visit to Steepleton Horse Fair along with a fine string of new horses. I had nothing to call my own, not even a name, except for the wretched garments I was wearing and in my hair a piece of scarlet ribbon.

I had ridden from Steepleton on the saddle of one of the grooms, but Mr Ogilvy himself chose to carry me into the house, which he entered from the stables through the kitchen. Coming then upon Mrs Duckham, the cook, he tossed me into her arms; as she was later to assure me, I was a wet and stinking bundle, and therefore with a shriek she promptly dropped me on to the white scrubbed floor where I lay, without moving, gazing up at her.

"Lord have mercy," said Mrs Duckham.

She bent down and set me on my feet, touching me as little as possible. "But sir," she said. "What am I to do with it?"

"Do with it? Why, give it food, clothes, whatever it needs."

"Yes, sir," said Mrs Duckham, doubtfully. "What's your name?" she asked.

I made no answer. Perhaps I had already forgotten my name.

"Call her Harriet,"said Mr Ogilvy.

"Harriet Ogilvy?" asked Mrs Duckham.

"Good God, no," was the gentleman's reply. And then he put his hand on my head. "She's dark enough—we'll call her Harriet Dark."

"Well then," said Mrs Duckham. "No need to take fright, Harriet Dark. You're among friends."

Friends? What were friends if I did not know them? I looked her in the face and then I spat. A ball of spittle landed on her cheek.

She cried out. "You little—" Her hand went to strike me, but Mr Ogilvy had burst out laughing.

"What is this creature, sir?" asked Mrs Duckham, wiping her face. "Is it a child, or is it an animal?"

"More one than the other, I fancy," said Mr Ogilvy, still laughing. "At any rate, she cost me nothing and in a year or two you can use her about the house."

"Yes, sir, of course, sir," said Mrs Duckham. But the eye she turned upon me was indeed grim. She took me by the collar, gingerly, and led me away, calling to the kitchen maids to help her.

They drew me into the yard. It was a crisp, cold day in October and the water as it came out of the pump was icy cold. But they put me under it just the same and Mrs Duckham stood by watching, arms akimbo. "That's right," she said. "Wash it out of her." I screamed and yelled with all my might but they still held me there.

Hearing the noise, the grooms gathered round to watch. I lunged out to kick one of my tormentors and sidestepping to avoid the kick she splashed herself with mud. "You little varmint," she said.

"Go to it, Betsey," called one of the grooms, laughing; "she'll get the better of you else."

"It'll be the death of *her*, I shouldn't wonder," said another of the stablemen.

"And good riddance," said Mrs Duckham smartly. "What do we want with that sort of filth?"

"Master won't be best pleased," he replied. "He took quite a fancy to her."

"All right, all right," said Mrs Duckham, whether as a result of that remark or no. "Take her in now, girls, and get her dry."

I was carried back into the kitchen and rubbed with a cloth, so hard that my ears tingled and tears came into my eyes.

"Now then, little love," said Betsey, wiping my face more gently. "There's no need to carry on so."

What right had she to pity me? I sank my teeth into her hand. "You devil," she said, starting back. Devil? Yes, that was right. She would think a while before she came near me again, and that was what I wanted.

They dressed me in some old shawls. "What I do with these then, Mrs Duckham?" asked Betsey, pointing to the little heap of garments they had taken off me.

"Burn them," she replied. "They're good for nothing else."

The girl went to do as she was told; and there, on top of the pile, was the piece of red ribbon from my hair. I leapt upon it. "That's mine," I said. And those were the first words I uttered at Thirleby Hall. "That's mine—and I'll keep it."

"Can she keep it, Mrs Duckham?"

Mrs Duckham turned away. "Let her have it if she wants it, she's got nowt else," was the reply.

Wrapped in my shawls, my ribbon safe in my hand, I was put to sit on a stool in a corner of the kitchen. "Here, have this," said Betsey and put a bowl of porridge upon my lap.

I was very hungry, I knew; but what was this porridge? I looked down at it. "Go on," she said. "It won't bite you," and bent down to take the spoon and feed me with it. I grabbed the spoon from her and thrust it into my mouth, only to drop it the next moment with a howl of pain for it was boiling hot. "Slowly," she said, laughing. I glared at her and thrust another boiling spoonful between my lips. The pain was worth it, just to see the silly, gaping look upon her face.

"Here, Betsey," said Mrs Duckham. "There's work for you," and being called she went away and left me to eat in peace. Once she had gone I ate the porridge in little morsels, bit by bit, and it soon became cooler. Then, it was not unpleasant.

I cannot remember now where I came from—it is as if I was born in the kitchen of Thirleby Hall. I was sure I had never been in such a place before. It was the biggest room I had ever seen, lit by oil lamps which did not reach into the corners so that I could not, that evening, see all there was to see. All around the walls hung frying pans and saucepans, huge, gleaming utensils, which I was later to do my share of scouring. In the middle of the room there were long wooden tables laden with dishes of all kinds, bowls and platters. And along one side was an enormous range presided over by Mrs Duckham herself, tasting from the pots on the fire with a long ladle, prodding here, slicing there. From the range there rose smells in profusion, of soups and broths, of fish steaming, roasts spitting. I watched Mrs Duckham and the kitchen maids at work and little by little I ate my porridge.

Presently the hurly burly of activity subsided. By then I was nodding on my stool and the kitchen maids at their work had become vast figures joined in some intricate dance, the movements of which I did not understand. I shuddered awake suddenly to see that they were all, thirty or more of them, Mrs Duckham, the kitchen maids, the grooms and others, sitting across the room at a long table. Through some mysterious sense of being watched I had awoken, for they had all turned to stare at me.

"Seems a shame, doesn't it?" one of them said to me, smiling. "Where's your mam, then, where's your mam?"

I opened my mouth and began to scream. Whereupon they got up from the table, some of them, and began to comfort me.

"That child," said Mrs Duckham pointing her knife in my direction,"is nothing but an animal. Mark my words."

"And who is the child?" asked a voice—one I had not heard before.

The maids began curtseying and I stopped my screaming in order to perceive the strange new figure. As I was later to discover, it was Mrs Minim, housekeeper of Thirleby Hall. She appeared very tall, especially as she was dressed from head to toe in shiny black. One large and shapeless foot came very near to mine and then she bent down and I saw that her face was very white and her teeth were yellow. Her hands were edged with black ruffles. One of those hands grasped me by the shoulder and forced me to be still, looking up at her.

"The master brought her," sniffed Mrs Duckham. "He found her at Steepleton Fair."

"I see," said Mrs Minim. "Abandoned, I suppose."

"I've no doubt of it," said Mrs Duckham. "She's a bad one, all right. What did she do first thing in the house but spit on me—and me offering her the hand of friendship."

"Bad, thoroughly bad," pronounced Mrs Minim. "Has she a name?"

"None of her own," said Mrs Duckham.

They all looked at me then with, I felt, renewed loathing and contempt. What could be made of a small child with no mother to care for her and not even a name to call her own? I had had a name once, certainly I had had a name, but now I could not for the life of me bring it to mind; and what name could such a bad creature have? I bent my head in shame.

One of the kitchen maids spoke up. "The master has given her a name, ma'am," she said. "He said to call her Harriet Dark."

"Harriet Dark?" said Mrs Minim. "A strange name. But if she has no other—" She turned away. "Let the child be put to bed," she said. "In the morning we can find some work for her."

Chapter Two

I AWOKE suddenly in the night. It was quite dark in the room and at first I could see nothing; but then little by little the outlines of the room became clear, the narrow, bare outlines, broken only by a chest of drawers in one corner and a small window high up on one wall.

Outside the dark was quite silent. Nothing was stirring, nothing seemed to be alive. I strained my ears for some sound and then caught suddenly the jarring call of a nightbird, winging its way across the empty parkland.

The voices of the previous evening came back into my mind. "She's nothing but an animal." "She's a bad one, all right." I felt my own blackness as if it had been soot, clinging to me, forcing its way down my throat. Yet it wasn't true—I knew that it wasn't true. My mother had loved me and I had loved my mother; between us there had been a great deal of love. She had called me—what was it?—her pretty one, her darling. Although I still could not remember my name as she had given it to me.

I put out my hand, searching for her. I knew that I had only to touch her dress, her hand, her arm to know reassurance. Where was she now? Could she, by some magic, have come back?

My hand touched a wide, rounded back, a warm back. I touched it gently, hoping for a moment that it could be hers. But I knew that it was not. A name came to me, the name of

Betsey, the kitchen maid. "All right, she can come in with me." Horrid Betsey who had laughed at me and stared, like the others. As much as the narrow bed would allow, I edged myself away and lay staring out at the darkness.

My mother had not abandoned me because I was bad. But she had not been able to keep me either. She had gone and I knew that she would not now come back. I felt like a dead tree felled by some huge and unexpected blow, lying with its branches in the mud, longing for the clear light of the sky, the soft embrace of the wind. The terror of the loneliness, the horror of the blow was too much; I gave a sudden, desperate scream.

The night shivered and broke. "What, what's this?" asked Betsey. I turned on her like the animal they had said I was and punched and kicked her with all my might.

The door opened and Mrs Duckham stood there, a candle in her hand. "Betsey? What on earth?"

Betsey, by this time, had tumbled out of bed and was keeping as far away from me as she could. "Whatever's the matter with the child—is she demented?" For answer I roared and sobbed and tore at the bed clothes with my teeth.

Mrs Duckham came over and took me by the shoulder. "What is it, child?" she said. "What's the matter?" Then she sat down on the edge of the bed. "Misses her mother, I've no doubt," she said.

I drew back at that, baring my teeth. The candle in her hand was throwing vast wavering shadows against the wall behind. With her moonlike face and hair straggling down from beneath her cap she looked like some monster of the night which, by my screaming, I had conjured up.

"Eh," she sighed. "We'd best leave her to herself. Come along, Betsey, you can finish the night with me. She'll be calm by the morning."

Monsters of the night were one thing, but to be left alone was another, a far worse horror. I lay stricken as the two women, taking the candle, went out of the room, shutting the door firmly behind them. Come back, I wanted to say, come back—but I could not utter the words. Speechless and appalled I strained my eyes and ears through the darkness to see, to hear. But there was nothing to see, no one to hear.

The first rays of the sun filtered in at last and gradually the room became light. As the attic walls became clear I fell asleep.

Chapter Three

BUT MRS DUCKHAM began as she meant to go on and hardly had I fallen asleep than I was shaken by the shoulder and told in unmistakable tones that it was time to get up. Shivering, I got into the clothes I had been left the night before and went down to the kitchens. And as I went, I got some idea, as I had not done the night before, of the size of the establishment at which I had arrived; for we went down flight after flight of narrow back stairs from what seemed to me to be the top of a mountain until we arrived at last at the ground floor and the large kitchen where the raking out of the ranges had already begun.

My job, as I was roughly told, was to make myself useful and as a start I was told to sweep up the dead ash. Then, whilst one range was lit the others had to be black-leaded and polished. I made a poor job of mine. "Here," said one of the maids in the end and, sighing, she pushed me aside and spat generously onto the hob. Her skin was gray, her hair was gray, but with ash, I soon realized, for she was not much older than I was myself.

When all was in order Mrs Duckham arrived downstairs, sighing and sniffing. "As for you, you little devil," she said to me, one arm raised. I dodged swiftly aside. "Keep out of her way's the best," said one of the maids to me. "She's always the same till she's had her breakfast."

And what of my breakfast? I watched hungrily from a corner as a feast was prepared for Mr Ogilvy; but for us in the kitchen there was only bread and milk, although in generous quantities.

And yet, having eaten, I felt better—heavy-eyed but able to perceive that this new life into which I had been thrown had some advantages, the advantage for example of large amounts of food, even if it did not arrive very frequently.

After breakfast there was the clearing up. I was put at one of the sinks with an enormous pot to clean. I washed it well enough, I thought; but, "Oh no, my girl," said Mrs Duckham firmly. "It must look like that," and she pointed with a righteous finger to the shining pans which lined the wall. I looked from one to the other; from the blackened pot I was trying to clean to the shining brass utensils I could see around me; it seemed impossible that one could ever resemble the other. But Mrs Duckham was standing over me, so I set to again.

But as I scoured, in a corner of the large dark room, so I became aware of the light and sunshine and air outside. The door into the stableyard was open; the grooms passed in and out and men came in from the fields with large bundles of vegetables and game for Mrs Duckham. All were duly inspected and put away by the maids, but no one seemed to have an eye for the late autumn sunshine, the cool air. We were like creatures underground, burrowing down, scurrying through the underground passages; and yet what sense did that make when outside light and sun awaited us?

One of the garden boys arrived with a basket of carrots. They were small and spindly. "And what am I to do with these?" inquired Mrs Duckham wrathfully, shaking a bundle of the things in the boy's face. At his reply a burst of laughter went up; and under cover of it I slipped along the wall and out of the door.

But Mrs Duckham was not as much distracted as I had thought. "Harriet!" she called. And then more loudly, "Harriet!" At that I ran for all I was worth and almost at once toppled over the feet of one of the grooms.

"Is this what you're wanting, Mrs Duckham?" he said.

"Little devil, I don't want her. But the master says she's to stay and there's an end to it. Now look here, you," she said. "The people here work. If they don't work, they don't eat, and you're the same as the rest of them."

The groom's hand was on my arm. For answer to Mrs

Duckham I bit into it—hard. As he yelped with pain, Mrs Duckham took a vigorous swipe at me, almost toppling over as I dodged away. "All right," she said as I ran. "You'll find out what I mean, I promise you that."

And there I was, in the open air. Once away from the kitchens and the stables beyond, I settled down to explore the new world with interest, for I had seen nothing like it before.

It was a vast and well-ordered kingdom that lay behind the mansion of Thirleby Hall. Everything was large, everything was neat. The stables, horses' heads appearing at every box, were freshly washed and swept and beyond them lay acre upon acre of kitchen garden, onions lying out to dry, trees well pruned, bushes tamed. I had known before straggling hedgerows, fields high with grass and buttercups; here were rows of vegetables laid out in straight neat lines.

It was not at all the countryside as I had known and loved it; but still it spoke to me of the life I had known and loved, for there were birds and the fresh smells of growing things. Away from the warmth of the kitchen ranges, the smell of the greasy pots, I felt myself again, not a dark creature of dirt and grime but a being light as air, as full of music as a blackbird or a linnet.

Once I had left the outbuildings behind me there were only the gardeners at work and although they looked at me with curiosity they did not stop to ask what I was about. As best I could I kept my distance from them. I had, at the back of my mind, the idea that if only I could walk far enough I could leave Thirleby Hall and go back to where I had come from, although I had only the vaguest idea of where that was. But as I walked on, I realized how difficult a task that would be; for it seemed beyond my capacities that morning even to reach the limits of the grounds.

I sat down at last to rest on a grassy verge. On the far side of the plot a solitary gardener worked, digging potatoes; I watched him, sucking a piece of grass, as he cut into the ground with his spade, pulled up the root and shook it clean of the earth.

He came close to me at last although he still did not look in my direction. I knew him though; he had been at table the night before and had witnessed my humiliation at the hands of Mrs Minim; I got up to walk on.

But before I could do so his words stopped me.

"Come with Mr Ogilvy, did you?" he said.

"Yes," I replied. His tone was more friendly than I had expected and so were his words. He had asked if I had "come with Mr Ogilvy" as if the choice had been mine.

"Going to stay then, are you?" he said next.

I glowered down at the newly turned earth—as black as the heart I carried within me for the hatred I bore every one of the folk I had found at Thirleby Hall.

"Don't know," I said at last.

"Reckon as how you should," he said. "You'll be all right here."

All right? Without my mother? Fed, no doubt, and watered, scrubbed and given clean clothes, but the nourishment I wanted only my mother could give me; and to find her I had to leave Thirleby Hall.

Then he said, "Come on, here's a job for you," and he gave me a root to shake clean of the dirt.

This was work too but work after my own heart, to put the potatoes whole and as clean as I could make them in the basket he provided. And as I worked, there were all the creatures of the earth to examine, the grubs, the earwigs, the worms. "Get a move on," urged the gardener whenever he got too far ahead; reluctantly I followed him.

At last he said, looking up at the sun, "Well, should be dinnertime." I was glad to hear that for I was, I realized, very hungry. He carried the vegetables we had dug and I walked cheerfully in his wake back to the house.

In the kitchen a grim voice greeted me. "So you're back then, are you," said Mrs Duckham; "when there's food about." Without being told, I went to the sink to scrub at my earth-blackened hands. I also saw, as I had not previously noticed, that dirt from the potatoes had gone on to the makeshift costume I was wearing. But there was nothing I could do about that. I went to sit at the far end of the table, as far away from Mrs Duckham as I could manage.

Again the kitchen was full of smells, good smells of meat and steaming vegetables. Mouth watering, I waited for my portion. Mrs Duckham was generous with the helpings I could see, looking at the big plates of food which were coming down the table. Next to me Betsey, elbows akimbo, was already, as though ravenous, shoving a large piece of beef into her mouth, washing it down with beer. There was nothing for me to drink; so I sat gripping the knife and fork before me, my stomach aching with hunger as I waited.

"And this is for *her*," said Mrs Duckham's voice, suddenly loud. There was a silence; and then I heard a few tittering sounds as a plate was handed towards me down the table. What could be on it, I wondered.

"Here," said Betsey; and shoved the plate at me so hard that what was on it almost fell into my lap. There was none of the meat, vegetables, good gravy with which her own plate was laden; there was instead a bone—and an old, dried bone at that.

"Well, she looks like a dog and all," came a voice from further up the table. I bent my head for a moment, the tears starting into my eyes; and then into that grieving emptiness came anger, rage even; I was being treated like an animal and yet I was in a place to which I had come through no wish of my own.

Holding the plate I marched the length of the room to Mrs Duckham. Glowering, she pretended not to see me coming but went on filling up the pile of plates before her.

"What's this?" I said.

She set down her knife.

"I told you," she said. "And I meant it. There's no food here for those who won't work."

I glared at her, prepared once more to spit, kick, stamp; but as I lifted my head I caught the smell from the platter before her, a glorious smell of roast meat. My stomach pulled with hunger and before I could prevent it, my eyes filled with tears. As we looked at each other, she as angry as myself, a calm voice came from down the table. "I don't know what all the fuss is about, I'm sure I don't. Hasn't the lass been working with me half the morning?"

"What?" said Mrs Duckham.

It was the gardener who had spoken. "It's as I say," he said, looking benignly across at me. "She worked with me digging the potatoes and a good worker she was and all."

"Hm," said Mrs Duckham and looked at me.

My head was hung well down by now, the tears falling in two thick streams down my cheeks.

"Hm," said Mrs Duckham again and took my plate from me. "Right then—here you are."

She put on it a generous slice of meat, potatoes and gravy. "For them that work," she said, "there's food in plenty."

"She's a good little picker and no mistake," said the gardener.

My tears had dried. Proudly I marched back down the room with my loaded plate and I ate until I thought my stomach would burst.

Chapter Four

THIS WAS the first of many struggles which took place between Mrs Duckham and myself, through which we came to have for each other a certain wary respect. "She's not such a bad little thing—at least not as much as she seemed at first," was Mrs Duckham's judgment after a few days. By then I had come to tolerate if not understand her insistence on work and cleanliness and the other concepts of how to be a good servant. I understood that I was to carry out at least some of the tasks she gave me and as far as I knew how I tried to keep myself neat and tidy. At the same time I knew that in return I would be kept well fed and warm. She would offer me no affection, but affection, I still insisted, I did not want.

However, sometimes in the evenings I would sit on the floor close to her chair, observing her fat hands with their red, tight skin and the wedding ring sunk deep into the flesh of one finger; and I would feel then that, sharp-tongued, abrupt as she was, her presence did hold some comfort.

One evening as we sat like this before the fire I asked her how long I had been there.

"Two weeks it must be," she said.

"How long is two weeks?" I asked.

She laughed. "Why it's twice times seven, of course. Here—seven." And she drew seven lines on the hearth with the poker.

I looked at the lines. There seemed to be a lot of them.

"Your home's here now," she said. "Your mother will have forgotten you by now."

My mother? For a moment a face came into my mind's eye and at the same time I heard a voice, but so briefly. Who had she been? As I struggled to find the face, the voice again, so a feeling rose, a longing within me. I could not find my memories of my mother and yet just the mention of her was enough to bring out a most powerful longing.

My heart felt like a stone as I looked down at the lines in the ashes of the hearth and the words of Mrs Duckham echoed in my ears. "She'll have forgotten you by now, for sure."

She hadn't forgotten me and she wasn't going to forget me. I wouldn't let her.

I lay on my back that night in bed, listening to Betsey snoring, and making my plans. I knew that Mr Ogilvy had brought me to Thirleby Hall from Steepleton Fair. Obviously enough then the thing to do was to find my way back to the fair. By now, I felt sure, my mother was looking for me and although I could not be sure that I would recognize her, I knew that she would know me.

I got up early the next day as I had done every day since that first morning and worked harder than usual at my early morning tasks. For breakfast there was bread and milk as usual; I ate with appetite, and as I did so, I thought about my plan and felt for the first time a small misgiving. How far was it to the fair? How long would it take to get there? For a time, I was sure, I could keep alive by eating what I could find along the way, but would I starve before ever I got there?

I looked round the kitchen and found that I liked it more than I had understood. The housemaids, the gardeners, the grooms, all of them accepted me now and left me alone to please myself. And that was all I wanted of them. Everything else that I wanted, my mother had to give me. And one day I would have it from her.

My courage returned to me. When breakfast was done I got up from the table and without so much as a glance of farewell I set off. In my pockets I had some vegetables that I had managed to save—and my piece of scarlet ribbon.

I went through the stables, past the gardens. I had earned the right by now to go where I chose in the nether regions of Thirleby Hall and no one stopped me. Only my first friend the gardener raised a hand in greeting as I went past.

I almost stopped then and my step slackened. But the will to find my mother carried me past. I wanted no substitutes.

It took me longer than I expected to leave the grounds of Thirleby Hall and penetrate the woods which lay behind it. I took out one of my carrots and bit into it to give myself cheer. From the house the woods did not look deep but they were dense and as I trudged on, my feet sinking into the soft earth of the path, I could not feel quite certain that I was going straight through it. I walked on without any way of knowing whether I was near the edge or not; and then, triumphant, I realized that I had somehow traversed the wood for I came to an open path, with the side of the valley rising steeply behind it.

Which way was I to go? Never mind which. I would walk on until I came across other travellers.

By now my vegetables had gone and I had seen only a few berries around me that I could eat. But I felt sure that soon I would come across a cottage, a house. I continued to walk along the track.

Suddenly, in the distance, I saw a group of riders coming towards me. My first thought was to hide, but then I thought that if I hid I would never know my way. So, boldly, I continued to walk on.

They came rapidly towards me and as they drew near I turned and waved so as to stop them. They seemed ready to go past; but then I heard a voice, a familiar voice. "Stop, stop." Looking upwards I saw the face of Mr Ogilvy.

"What's this? You're far from home," he said.

I looked sullenly at my feet for a moment but then I made up my mind to tell him the truth. "I'm not staying with you," I said. "I'm going to my mam."

He got down from his horse. Yet even then he seemed a mile high; my eyes came to rest on his legs, wide, sturdy legs like the trees I had just passed through.

"So you're leaving us," he said. "What's your name again?"

"Harriet," I said. "Harriet Dark—it's the name you gave me."

"Yes," he said thoughtfully. "You're looking for your mother, are you, Harriet Dark? Do you know the way to go?"

For answer I pointed with my head onwards along the track.

"It's a long way," he said. "Further than you know." And something in his tone of voice made me shiver just for a moment; but then once more I plucked up my courage.

The next thing after that I was caught up and placed on his

saddle. Then he put his horse to the gallop.

I kicked, I struggled, but it was no use. "Stay still," he commanded. "Or you'll do both of us a mischief." And so I stayed still in the end and was brought back to Thirleby Hall.

That evening, as I was sitting playing in the ashes of the hearth with a little bit of stick, Mrs Minim came into the kitchen. "Where is the child?" she asked. "Mr Ogilvy wishes to see the child."

"Heavens above, just look at her," was Mrs Duckham's reply. I was caught up and thoroughly scrubbed and brushed, protesting all the time.

Mrs Minim stood at the door while this was going on, her lips thin. "Be thankful it's us you're dealing with, not her," said Betsey into my ear. "She's the devil incarnate when she's a mind to be."

But that did not frighten me; I was at home with devils. Was I not myself, as Mrs Duckham told me several times a day, a devil's child?

By this time I knew the back of the house, the kitchens, the pantries, the storerooms well enough, as indeed I knew the gardens, stables and outhouses. But I had never before penetrated to the front of the house. It was to the front of the house that Mrs Minim now conducted me.

Swiftly she walked away from the big, friendly kitchen with its cheerful noise and down a long corridor. It felt as if we were walking into the depths of the earth. She whisked suddenly, skirts rustling, around a corner, taking the lamp with her and my heart pounding I ran to catch her up, feeling that if I lost her I would never find her again. I ran into her full tilt, for she had stopped to open a door.

We were in the strangest place I had ever seen, a great long hall which stretched before me, wide and empty. Beneath my feet the floor, cold, was made of stone and above my head walls went on and on, up to a very high ceiling. Mrs Minim went confidently forward, the lamp in her hand; and suddenly into the little pool of light came a white, still face.

I think, then, I almost fainted; certainly I gasped, so loudly that Mrs Minim stopped in her tracks. "Sssh, child," she said.

I pointed into the darkness. "What's that?" I asked.

She raised the lamp and once more the pale face with its cold, dead eyes came into view. I shuddered and clutched at her skirt, but she pulled impatiently away from me. "That?" she said. "It's a statue, of course."

"A statue?" What was "a statue"? Woods, hedgerows and open fields held no terrors for me. But what on earth was a statue?

She took my hand in hers. Her fingers felt as cold and dead in mine as the face we were looking at. "Touch it," she said, and drew my hand towards it.

I screamed then, once, twice and then a third time, my arm rigid with terror as I tried to draw back. Whatever the thing was, it was dead. I remembered suddenly another dead face that I had seen, which I had touched and found cold where I had expected to feel it warm; and I had screamed then too and someone had come running and snatched me away. "There, there, poor child. There, there."

And again now someone came. On the far side of the empty hall a door was flung open. "Mrs Minim?" said a voice, a mild voice but a voice of authority. "My orders were to bring the child here, not to kill her with fright."

How reduced then was the power of the majestical Mrs Minim! "I'm very sorry, sir," she said, bobbing a curtsey. "The child was frightened by the statues, sir."

"Yes, yes, no doubt. Now leave us alone, will you?"

The room I found myself in was also strange; but I concluded in an instant that it was the most beautiful room I had ever seen. Under my feet there was a thick, warm carpet, woven in a pattern of rich blues and reds; there were more lamps than I had ever seen together, many more than we had to cook by in the kitchen, and each lamp glowed upon some object which I instantly longed to touch so as to feel with my own hands the rose-red wood, the glittering crystal. I stood stockstill, gazing round; and then I saw that against the dark wood of the walls hung pictures, of ladies in feathered hats, of horses, dogs and, too, of children. I looked up at these dainty creatures, their pink cheeks, clear eyes and hair which looked as if it had never been tangled; I would have given anything in that instant to have been one of those children.

Mr Ogilvy was standing at the far end of the room before the hearth. A log fire was burning behind him; so, I thought, must look the devil himself before the fires of hell, so big was he, so broad, with the flames flickering and rising at his back. And then he said, "Come here, child"; and I could not move.

There was a silence. "Frightened half out of its wits," I heard him mutter; then he turned to sit down in the chair before the fire, stretching out his legs before the blaze. "The fire," he remarked to no one in particular, "is a kind thing on a night such as this."

He had reminded me of how cold I was. And so, carefully, inch by inch, almost, I edged my way up the room past all the tables, the chairs, the pictures and the rugs which were strewn, as if by some careless, lavish hand, across the carpet. And I came to the fire at last, but not daring to go too close either to its warmth or to the recumbent figure of Mr Ogilvy, even though, one hand across his eyes, he appeared to have forgotten that I was still in the room.

And then at last he said in a quiet, mild voice, "Well, then." I jumped back at that; but he did not turn his head in my direction and so, after a moment, I crept back again to where the warmth of the fire reached me; and I stretched out my hands to the blaze.

He said,"I suppose you do not know why I brought you here."

No, I did not know; but neither did I want to know. I was sure by now that the world considered me quite evil; he must have found me after some piece of wrong-doing, something so bad that I could not even remember it myself; something for which my mother had abandoned me. I said, "No, but don't, don't tell me."

He looked surprised at that and, I thought as I peeped at him, amused; how evil he must be himself, I thought, to laugh at evil in others. "I see," he said. "If you do not wish to hear, you need not. What I want you to understand is that if you run away, as you tried to do today, you will end up in the poorhouse—or worse."

The word "statue" had had no meaning for me. But the word "poorhouse" had plenty. Someone I had known, it must have been my mother, had feared the poorhouse more than anything, more even than death itself.

I said, "I was going to try to find my mother."

"And you were fortunate indeed that I found you before you had got very far. Most likely you would have been lost in the woods and would have died of hunger otherwise."

"That's not true," I said. "Not true." And yet I felt that perhaps it was the truth; for by the time I got back to Thirleby Hall that afternoon I had been very hungry indeed and glad of the scraps of bread I had found to feed on before suppertime.

"I think you do understand," he said.

He was smiling; when he smiled, the satanic cast of his

features was lost completely; he looked benevolent, agreeable even. But I refused to smile back at him for this man, I was convinced of it, was my enemy; he had taken me away from the only love I had ever known and that he should not have done, for whatever reason. Because of that, and I resolved it there and then, I would hate him for the rest of my life. One day, when I was bigger, stronger, able to do my own will, I would show him my hate.

"Well now," he said again in the same comfortable tone of voice. "You must go back to the kitchens where you belong."

"Where you belong." Yes, I thought, the evil creature he thought I was certainly did not belong in this warm, well-lit room; and yet I rebelled against his words just the same.

I said, "Don't belong there—I belong—"

And then I paused. For I could not think where I belonged, except outside, where I could run and jump and cast off the darkness, the entangling hate which here at Thirleby Hall threatened to choke me a hundred times a day.

He yawned. Oh, how at ease he looked there in his armchair, sure, of course, where *he* belonged—in warmth and comfort. He said, "You may not belong there by rights. But the kitchen is the only place for you at the moment."

I looked around me, at the rich hangings of red silk, at the big open fire. I said, "It's better here."

"No doubt," he agreed. "But it's not for you."

I turned to go. But then I remembered the darkness of the hall and the staring face that it contained. I was afraid to go through that hall alone. I hesitated for a moment and then said in a voice that would tremble, "Sir, I..."

"Ah yes," he said; and I realized that he guessed what kept me back. How, I wondered, had he seen into my mind? When he got up from his chair I started away from him.

"You must not," he said, "be afraid of stone and marble. Believe me, from them you have nothing to fear. Let me show you."

I said, "I'm not touching anything!"

"Don't worry," he said. "I shall not ask you to." Again a smile crossed his face. "Now," he said. "If statues are so strange to you, I daresay paintings are too—and books. At Thirleby Hall there are plenty of all of these and you may as well know what they are."

He pointed to the chimney-piece. Above it there was a picture of a big tall man. "My grandfather," said Mr Ogilvy. "He collected many of the things you will see in this house. That is a portrait of him, painted by the artist Gainsborough." And then, as if listening to his own voice, he smiled to himself and muttered something I did not catch.

I was looking up at the face. What had he called it? A portrait, painted by an artist? What was a portrait, what was an artist? Was an artist a person like Mr Ogilvy?

"Are you an artist?" I asked.

"Heavens above," he said. "What a question. Come along, come along. I will show you a book and a statue and then your education, or as much as you will ever need of an education, will be complete."

He drew me to the tall shelves at the side of the room. "These are books," he said, and took down one of the objects on the shelves and opened it.

It was a big brown thing containing, I saw, thick white sheets. The sheets had a strange, mildewed smell and I wrinkled my nose at it. And what were the black marks on the sheets? I put out my hand to feel them.

"So," he said, "You're not frightened of *everything*."

"I'm not frightened of nothing," I told him emphatically, "except dead faces. And that thing in the hall was a dead face."

"Ah," he said. "I see."

I was feeling the black squiggles on the book, surprised that they were flat and not raised as I had expected them to be. "What is a book?" I asked.

"A book," said Mr Ogilvy as if to himself, "is everything or nothing. It contains all of life, or nothing of life. It tells you the truth—or it leads you astray. Books, to some men, are the cruellest will-of-the-wisps—leading men to waste their lives in useless effort to contain all of the life within them."

I did not know what he was talking about. "But what are these?" I asked, jabbing at the black marks with my fingers.

"They are words," he said.

"Words?"

"You speak in words. Long ago men found a way to write down the words they spoke so that they could be preserved."

He looked at me; I looked at him. I said, "I would like to know words."

"Yes, well, indeed," he said. "But now there is time for only one last lesson for you."

He picked up a lamp and led me out of the room. "I'm not going anywhere near it," I said.

"Better not, if you're going to scream again," he replied. But with the lamp in one hand he rested the fingers of the other against the face that had so frightened me. "Julius Caesar," he said. "The head of Julius Caesar, made out of stone. And a fine example."

"Is it dead?" I asked.

"Not as you mean it," he replied. "In the sense you mean, it was never alive." He gave the head an affectionate pat. "There. So off you go."

"Please sir, it's dark."

From nowhere that I had perceived her, Mrs Minim glided forward. "I'll take the child back, sir."

"Goodbye, Harriet," he said. And the door of the library closed behind him.

I went up to the statue and patted it as I had seen Mr Ogilvy do. "It's not dead," I said disdainfully to Mrs Minim; "it's never been alive."

Chapter Five

AT THAT I thought Mr Ogilvy would have forgotten me; but he did not, or at least not immediately, as I found out a few days later.

I was in a corner of the kitchen, scraping off the breakfast dishes. Suddenly there was quiet; and I looked up to see Mr Ogilvy standing in the doorway, his shadow stretching far into the room. "Good morning, Mrs Duckham," he said as she curtseyed and all the kitchen maids imitated her, bowing and dipping as if before the wind. I did not curtsey, but continued with my work.

"Is she here?" he asked. "Is the child here?"

"Yes, sir," said Mrs Duckham. "Harriet!"

I was shoved forwards until I stood in front of Mr Ogilvy. In that moment I became aware of how dirty I was; that my hair was straggling downwards, that my hands were grimed. I remembered the sweet, fairfaced children who lined the walls of Mr Ogilvy's library and again I wished to be one of them.

"Hm," he said as he looked at me. "You must see to her clothes, Mrs Duckham."

"Her clothes?" Mrs Duckham was surprised. "But sir—"

"Mrs Duckham?"

There was a pause during which if my hands had not already been icecold with the water I was using for the dishes, they would most certainly have frozen. Mr Ogilvy, it was said, was a man who did not tolerate argument and this I was now seeing for myself. I remembered the gentleness he had shown towards me a few evenings before and I marvelled at it.

And then he said to me, "This is for you." He put his hand in his pocket and took out a small squirming object.

It was a very young kitten, a few inches long only. It was white all over and, I saw as it opened its eyes, its eyes were as bright as the bluest sky I had ever seen.

"Do you want it?" he asked me.

"Oh yes," I said.

"Well then, have it, care for it." And he turned on his heel and swept back into the stable yard. A moment later he and the grooms were gone.

The maids crowded round me and only Mrs Duckham stood back. "It's one of that white cat's litter," she said. "The only one left. A fox took the rest and the mother as well—happen it won't live, especially with her to look after it."

The little creature was scrabbling frantically in my hands, mewing. "It'll be hungry," said Betsey. "Let me take it." But I pressed the animal against me. "I'll feed it," I said. "What should I give it?"

"Listen to little high and mighty," said Mrs Duckham. "Clothes indeed! What does she want clothes for? Now get to your work, all of you." She had something else to blame me for now, the irritation of Mr Ogilvy. Easily angered, she turned back to her table with a face like fire and began slapping newly-made dough against the wood as if it were something alive that she hated.

I whispered to Betsey, "What should I do?"

"Give it a bit of warm milk," she said. "Here," and she showed me how to feed the tiny creature by dropping milk into its mouth for it was too small even to lap.

My life in the kitchen was changed from that day. The kitten stayed with me as I worked and when in the evening I sat by the hearth it snuggled into my lap. To be sure, I had to be careful to keep it out of Mrs Duckham's way; for if she came across it she would aim a hearty kick at it; but it soon learned of its own accord to be wary.

At night the kitten slept with me, for I took it upstairs hidden in the bodice of my dress. By now I had dresses of my own made for me by the sewing maids. They were of a thick material which scratched my skin and they had been cut over-generously to allow for growth, but they were my own clothes.

As I slept, the kitten lay curled against my neck; and while I slept with her my dreams were pleasant ones.

Then, one day, it was lost. Mrs Duckham had sent me on an errand to the far kitchen garden with a message for my old friend, the gardener.

"Mrs Duckham says, what cabbage have you got, because she must have some," I said.

He leant on his spade and considered. "Sit down there, little lass," he said at last; "and we'll see what we can find."

He cut the cabbage for me with a knife he had about him and piled up several large ones in my arms. "Now take care," he advised; "they're fine plants and she won't want them damaged." So I walked slowly back to the house.

It was a cold day and soon the hands that held the cabbages before me were red and stiff. And yet I cast a longing look behind me at the brooding sky, the trees, their bare branches motionless in the still air before I went again into the kitchen, away from the outside world where I felt I belonged.

Mr Ogilvy was entertaining guests to luncheon. Such events always put Mrs Duckham into a frenzy and this day was no exception. We were all worked hard; I knew that the little cat was not at my side, but it was not until the afternoon that I had leisure to search for her.

She was nowhere to be found. "How should I know?" asked Mrs Duckham when I dared to question her. "Maybe she ran outside." I looked in the stableyard, but I could see no sign of her.

It was Betsey who found her in the end, Betsey who had been sent down to the cellar for a jar of vinegar. One of the footmen went with her to hold the lamp; and there under the stairs leading up to the cellar door they found my kitten, quite dead.

I knew by then that it must have died, for it had been away for so many hours. If it had stayed with me, it would never have died; but Mrs Duckham had sent me outside and while I was away it had ventured into the cellar and fallen against its head.

Mrs Duckham chose to point the moral of the occasion. "Why Mr Ogilvy bothered with you I shall never understand," she said. "Anyone could have seen you weren't worth the bothering."

I looked up from the scrap of white fur in my lap and my anger and grief at its dying came together in an overwhelming impulse of rage. "Mr Ogilvy?" I said. "I *hate* Mr Ogilvy."

Mrs Duckham was ready for me there—she screamed till she was blue, belabouring me meantime about the head. I kicked her back and punched her as best I could, but then Harry the groom came in. He picked me up, carried me out and threw me into a shed at the far end of the kitchen garden.

I fell on to some straw. The place was dark, for it was night, and there was a strong smell of dung. I knew I was to be left to spend the night there, but I refused to cry to be let out; for to do that would have given them satisfaction and that I would not do. Besides nothing mattered to me then except that my kitten was dead.

I must have slept at last, for I woke to a feeling in my arm like a sharp pinch. There it was again—and again, much harder this time. I cried out with the pain and swung my arm up. Something was hanging from it, something with eyes which gleamed red in the darkness. I screamed then and flung the creature up and away from me, hearing it thud against the back wall of the shed. Then I crawled as far as I could away from it to stand shuddering against the other wall.

I stood there for what seemed like many hours, for what must have been many hours, for when at last the door opened and in came the blessed light I fell over on to the straw and had to be carried back to the house.

Harry put me down before the fire and they all gathered round to look at me. Mrs Duckham said, "So you see, you young devil." But her voice was not as firm as I had been used to hearing it.

I said nothing, but put my hand over the place on my arm where the creature of the dark had bitten me. I would tell no one, for I wanted no one's pity.

As I continued to sit in silence the maids moved back to their work. It was all forgotten, it seemed, and by dinnertime Mrs Duckham herself appeared to have forgotten it, for she served me my usual portion, not more to make up for the starvation I had suffered and not less to continue my punishment.

Of the kitten there was no sign; the small body had been swept up and away with the rest of the kitchen debris.

But my hatred had not disappeared; rather it had grown inside me until I could feel it, large, hard and cold like the head of Julius Caesar. I felt that I too had become an artist; my tool was privation, my creation was hate.

Chapter Six

FOR A WHILE then the world was very dark. The years passed, as they had to do; I did not know when my birthday was but I knew that spring succeeded winter, summer spring, and all that I did was work hard, rising early with the birds and going to bed at night too tired except to sleep heavily without dreams. I grew, I must have done. I ate, I washed pots and I swept floors as I had done since my arrival at Thirleby Hall but now I did not for a moment look beyond my daily life for the joy that had once illuminated it. No whitehaired kitten replaced the one I had lost and I did not think even of finding my mother again, so impossible did that seem. "The child's deaf," said Betsey, finding that I would respond only to a hefty clout; I knew that that was not true, but I could not explain even to myself why it was that her voice and Mrs Duckham's seemed always to come from very far away.

I remember even Mr Ogilvy from this time as a quite remote figure. I would glimpse him through the kitchen door mounting or dismounting from one of his horses, to me gigantic creatures; but I did not dream of speaking to him. The few words of friendship he had once spoken to me I had quite forgotten and so enclosed was I in my state of servitude that any relation between myself and that grand and distant figure, other than that of slave and master, was unimaginable.

I was living out a long winter; it lasted for several years. And yet, just as spring does follow winter, so at last did an awareness of the light return to me.

Mrs Duckham had sent me up to a farm on the estate with a message. "Hurry back, mind, there's work for you here," she urged. "Yes, Mrs Duckham," I said, knowing that there was no need for her to urge because in those days I always did what I was told without asking questions.

And yet on that day it was different.

I walked up through the woods, wrapped in a wool cloak over the cotton dress I wore in the house. I was always cold then and sometimes shivering; I remember that. But then as I walked over the damp earth I found myself noticing that the sun was after all warm and that there was no need for me to huddle within my cloak. What month was it, I asked myself, and seeing the budding leaves I knew that warm though the sunshine was it must still be spring.

But I walked on without stopping to the farm, not straying along the little paths as once I would have done, but walking on as straight as I knew.

I repeated Mrs Duckham's message to the farmer's wife who opened the door to me. "Mrs Duckham says as she needs the eggs."

The eggs had not been gathered. "You'll have to wait," said the woman and nodded me into the house to sit on a brown settle before the fire which was burning in spite of the warmth outside. I sat, hands clasped, eyes downcast; on the table in front of me there was a large yellow seed cake but I looked at it with indifference; I was not hungry.

The farmer's wife came back with the basket of eggs. She said, "You can have a piece of that cake if you wants it."

I looked at her in amazement. "Go on, let me cut you a slice," she urged. My eyes went back to the cake; and it seemed to me all of a sudden that I had never been so hungry in all my life as I was for a piece of that tall, thick, bright yellow cake; I felt my mouth running with saliva, my tongue longing to curl round its crumbs. The farmer's wife was cutting it. "Only a little one, as you don't seem too keen," she said. But then without asking me she put down a mug of milk to go with it.

No food had ever tasted so delicious to me. And yet I was still glad that the slice was a small one and that the mug of milk was only half full. For my empty stomach was full in a moment.

I managed to finish what was before me and then I stood up. "What do you say?" demanded the farmer's wife. "Thank you," I muttered, gazing down at the floor. Then I took the basket of eggs and ran out of the door and away from the farm as fast as I could.

But something had changed, I knew it; or rather I knew that something had begun to change. I walked rapidly back through the woods, not looking up at the sun or around me at the pale green which lined the trees. Then I smelt something and suddenly I had to stop, I could not go on.

In a little glade beside me, under an awning of beech boughs, there was a dense mass of bluebells. I looked at them with wonder and then dropping to my knees pushed my face into them so that the smell, the colour filled my nose, my eyes. In that moment it was as if some thick shrouding veil dropped from around me; I could see, smell, hear and touch as I had not been able to do for several years. I pulled handfuls of the flowers from the ground, crushing the thick, pale stems.

And as I did so there came a memory, a quick, tantalizing memory as if a veil within my mind was also being lifted. I heard a voice saying gently, sweetly, "Bluebells, what lovely bluebells," and my eyes filled with tears without my knowing why and I burst into sobs, my head thrust into the deep scent of the flowers.

I got back late from my errand and was sorely cuffed for my fault; yet I ate dinner that night with a good appetite. Some part of me which had died had come alive again that day through the spring, the seed cake of the farmer's wife and a profusion of bluebells. I was restored.

Chapter Seven

IN MY newly restored condition, which was not perfect but still a good deal preferable to the dungeon of grief in which I had spent the several previous years, I began to see that life at Thirleby Hall even for a drudge such as myself contained some entertainments and consolations.

The chief of these was the gardener who had been my first friend and champion, Mr Bennett. As I had done when I first arrived at Thirleby Hall I took again to wandering about the grounds whenever I could escape my work, and I found there Mr Bennett always at his slow and laborious tasks, a black clay pipe often unlit between his lips. I watched him as he worked, planting, digging, sowing, weeding. He loved the earth and often he would plunge a hand into the soil and let the dirt trickle down from between his fingers. One day, greatly daring, I did the same and I found that I too loved the feel of it clinging to my skin and I too loved its colour. "Ay, it's good earth," Mr Bennett would say contentedly and I agreed with him. Once I even tried licking it to discover its taste. "Lass, lass," said Mr Bennett in horror and as the flavour reached my taste buds I spat with vigour. But still I thought it looked nice enough to eat.

I came to love not only the earth but all the things which grew in it, the light green, feathery tops of the carrots, the copper-bright bunches of onions drying out against the ground. Mr Bennett grew flowers as well as vegetables; lilies, dahlias, chrysanthemums, great tawny masses of petals and leaves with the thick, dragging texture of the hassock on which I made my prayers in chapel. He would bring baskets of cut flowers into the kitchen for the decoration by Mrs Minim of the receiving rooms of the Hall and Mrs Duckham would exclaim in admiration at the sight they made. "You're a marvel, Mr Bennett, you really are." To which he always made the same reply: "Praise the Good Lord, not me."

"Don't touch them, you," she would say to me, accompanying the warning with a hard slap; and so I would keep my distance, staring till I thought my eyes would burst at the brilliant reds and oranges splashed across the table top and widening my nostrils like a horse to catch their heavy, drugging scent.

But if I was made to treat the garden flowers with an exaggerated respect—and even Mr Bennett would guard jealously these products of his labour—there was no one to stop me from seeking out the flowers which grew wild. Of these there were a multitude to be found, for they grew in every nook and cranny. My favourite remained the bluebell but at every season of the year there was something to be found of rare beauty, snowdrops, daffodils in the early spring, campion and wild thyme at the height of summer. Everywhere I could I feasted upon them.

And as I got to know the plants and the earth of the estate of Thirleby Hall, so also I came to know the animals in which the back regions of the house abounded, cats, dogs, chickens and especially horses. As passionately as Mr Bennett loved his flowers and vegetables, Harry the groom loved the horses; I loved them too and through this shared devotion I came to make friends with Harry.

At first I was very wary of getting too close to the horses; I was very small, they were very tall and I never knew for sure which way those great legs and feet were going to move. Neither did Harry and he had blackened toenails to prove it. But at the same time it was obvious that he was not afraid of them. All the time that he was brushing their coats, feeding them, he talked to them in a low, friendly voice.

I would watch from a safe distance. Through watching Harry I came to envy very much the friendship he seemed to enjoy with his animals. He never appeared to notice that I watched him at work, but he must have known it just the same, for one day when he was leading one of the horses out from the stall he said, as if to the air, "A beauty, isn't she?"

"Yes," I said, when no one else replied.

"Come and give her a pat," he said.

I moved cautiously round. "That's it," he directed. "Quietly, like that."

I put my hand on the broad firm nose. The horse stood quite still looking down at me and, made very bold, I patted her, looking up at the thick, straight eyelashes.

I said, "I should like to ride."

Harry laughed. "Who wouldn't? There's an old saying—if wishes were horses, beggars would ride."

"I'm not a beggar."

"Near as makes no difference."

Once, in response to words such as those, I would have kicked him in the shins. But I no longer kicked, or bit, or fought, except in my own mind; so I merely withdrew glowering to my former place against the wall.

Harry continued to stand by the horse. He said again as if to no one in particular, "The Good Book says pride goeth before a fall."

I said nothing. Harry, the friend of the horses, was no friend of mine; he was as bad as Mrs Duckham, or Mrs Minim, reminding me of my place, my obligations.

"There, there," said Harry to the mare. Then he looked across at me. "Have you seen the foal?" he asked.

I did not answer.

"You can see him if you want," he said.

I got up.

"Right," he said.

I walked behind him, not beside him, down the yard. He needn't think that I could be bought as easily as that, I thought, calling me a beggar. But then we came to the end stall and all I could see was the mother.

"I'll give you a lift," said Harry.

He put me on his shoulder so that I could see in to the stall. The foal, much bigger than I had expected, was leaning against the mother's side nudging into her, while the mother stood chewing the hay which was strewn about the floor. "Can I pat her?" I asked.

"You'd best not," said Harry, "she'd have your hand off. Not when she's just foaled."

I watched for a few more moments. How comfortable the two of them looked together, I thought. I said, "I wouldn't mind being a horse."

Harry grunted. "They've got more sense than humans, that's for sure." He put me back down on the ground. Then he said, "Do you still want to ride?"

"Oh yes," I said.

"Come on then."

He led me away from the stables down past the cabbages. "Where are we going?" I asked.

"You'll see," he said.

And there, her nose deep in a patch of thistles, was a donkey. "Up you go then," said Harry.

For a moment I was almost in tears. "You're laughing at me," I said at last.

"Me? Laughing?" said Harry.

I looked up at him. He wasn't laughing and it suddenly struck me that I could no more imagine him laughing than I could a horse. He had the same kind of long, sombre face with large, mournful eyes. No, Harry wasn't laughing at me.

He said, "You have to get used to animals, see. Now this donkey here's a good one."

He lifted me on to her back and I sat, legs stuck out on either side; then she moved forward and I fell forward, banging my nose on her head, clutching at her ears for support. "You see?" said Harry. "You have to hold on."

I nodded. The blow on my face had made my eyes tear but I was as proud as Punch nonetheless, sitting up on the donkey's back. Slowly she moved forward again, but this time I kept my balance.

When we got back to the stables I said to Harry, "Some day I'd like to ride a horse like that one." I pointed to Mr Ogilvy's favourite chestnut.

"You would and all," said Harry and drew the corners of his mouth far down. But there was no doubt about it after that day, he and I were friends, and I would scuttle about after him, just as I did after Mr Bennett, helping him with his tasks. From the donkey I progressed to an ancient pony and was even told, "You'd make a good little rider."

But he would not put me up on any of the best horses. "No, they're for the ladies and gentlemen," he said.

It was the thought of that which made me say, "I'll be a lady, one day."

"No, you won't," Harry contradicted firmly. "You've got to be born one, that's the only way. You see," he said, "it's like these horses. Now a donkey can no more be the kind of animal

Mr Ogilvy would ride, no more than fly. It's the breeding that counts—and the station in life you were born to."

I pondered this. Then I said, "That's not fair."

"Fair? What's fair got to do with it?"

I said, "Well, I don't see how you can be so sure. I may not be a lady now, but I don't see why I shouldn't grow up to be one."

He looked at me and I looked down at myself, at the skimpy cotton gown I was wearing, at my reddened hands. I thought for a moment he was going to laugh, but then he said quite gently, "You see, Hattie, if you was going to be a lady, you'd be getting ready for it now—you'd be learning to read, and things like that."

"Harriet," I said, "not Hattie." But I was thinking about what he had said, just the same. If learning to read was part of learning to be a lady—why then, I would learn to read.

Chapter Eight

IN FACT I knew very little indeed at that time about ladies or about what it meant to be a lady. Now I had two facts to conjure with: that ladies rode horses and that ladies could read. Otherwise I knew almost nothing about creatures who were so foreign to my world of the kitchen, the stable and the vegetable garden, except that I had seen ladies, real ladies, from time to time in the chapel of Thirleby Hall.

Mr Ogilvy was still unmarried and so there was no Mrs Ogilvy to give me an idea of what constituted a lady; but although Mr Ogilvy lived alone in that huge mansion with its troop of servants he did entertain from time to time quite large parties of ladies and gentlemen. As a kitchen maid I was not privileged to wait upon these grand personages, or even to visit the front part of the house in their presence; but I did see them at Sunday services in chapel.

The ladies, Mr Ogilvy's guests, appeared to me a truly amazing sight, as different from Mrs Minim, the only other person I knew who claimed to be something of a lady, as Mrs Minim was from me. They came rustling into chapel in full skirts of flowery pinks and yellows; around their shoulders they wore delicate lacy shawls with long fringes of silk and on their heads caps of all shapes and sizes. Around their pink cheeks were grouped fat, shining curls.

To me these visitors seemed scarcely human, just as by a sparrow a peacock will not be recognized as another bird; and indeed as they went past us their eyes would go over us as if they too scarcely saw us as belonging to the same species as themselves.

I remained in doting admiration of these creatures and dearly longed to know more about them. As the flock of ladies, heads bobbing, eyes cast demurely downwards, came to leave the chapel one evening, so one of them dropped a handkerchief. I was standing at the end of a pew waiting for them to pass; and quickly I picked up the handkerchief and hastened to restore it to its owner.

"Please, ma'am," I said.

The lady turned to look down at me with, beside her, Mr Ogilvy. I thought I had never seen such fine, pale skin, so delicately flushed with pink. "Please, ma'am," I said again, blushing this time, "your handkerchief."

I held out to her the scrap of white lace and even myself in that moment saw the incongruity of its being within my broad red hand. But still I was not prepared for her reply. "Oh pooh," she said, wrinkling her small, unfreckled nose. "Pray keep it do—I should not want it now."

The ladies moved away in a chattering, scented bevy. As I stood back, Betsey was on me in an instant. "What have you got here? I'll have it," she said.

I yielded it to her without a murmur, for I did not want it either.

What I did want was something much different and I was determined one day to have it. One day, I said to myself, one day when I was grown up I too would receive the recognition of a lady.

Chapter Nine

IT WAS clear that to reach my goal I needed a new rule of conduct. The first rule of life I had learned at Thirleby Hall was that as long as I did what I was told I would be fed, housed, and clothed. I would still be beaten about the head by Mrs Duckham from time to time to keep her hand in, as it were, but my life would be at a certain level perfectly tolerable. Suddenly this was not enough; I wanted something more than would in the normal course of events be offered to me, and I had to find a way of manipulating those around me so that they would allow me to have what I wanted.

It was necessary, first of all, to move my sights out of my immediate world. Harry knew all there was to know about horses and Mr Bennett knew all about plants but neither of them could read. In fact, apart from Mr Ogilvy the only persons of my acquaintance who could read, as far as I knew, were Mrs Minim and the Reverend Thomas Ponsonby, who came each Sunday from the nearby village of Swithindale to conduct the services in the family chapel.

By now I had been at Thirleby Hall for several years and I knew the Reverend Ponsonby and his sermons very well indeed. But I was not at all sure that he knew me, for in all these years of my faithful attendance at chapel, he had never addressed so much as a word to me. He came from Swithindale on horseback; and he would always begin the service with a scarlet face, his white hair in a ruffled circle round his head; but bit by bit, as the considerable chill of the ancestral chapel penetrated his cassock, it was his nose which took over as the most colourful feature of his face. Then, and we could rely on it, he would begin to gallop through the closing phases of the service, as if already preparing to make a flying leap on to his horse and return to Swithindale. It hardly seemed feasible to attract the attention of Mr Ponsonby in the brief space of time he spent each week at Thirleby Hall.

It seemed to me, therefore, that my only hope lay in gaining the favour and interest of Mrs Minim. In the ordinary way of things I had little to do with Mrs Minim, for I worked in the kitchen, which was controlled by Mrs Duckham, and my work rarely took me out of these back quarters as far into the house even as Mrs Minim's room. Mrs Minim herself came into the kitchen twice a day on average to give Mrs Duckham her instructions, but she ate her meals in her own room and did not usually mix with the lower servants.

However, what I did know of her, I thought I could well turn to my own advantage. She was genteel and she was pious; Mrs Duckham frequently lectured us as to how we should conduct ourselves and yet even more frequently she had to be helped up to bed. "Tired" she said she was; but it took little observation to see that she became tired very quickly after partaking in the beer that was brewed at the Hall, or in the wine which, on special occasions, was brought up from the cellar. Mrs Minim, stiffnecked in her black, I had never seen to be tired. I quickly decided that the way to ingratiate myself into Mrs Minim's favour, although undoubtedly as a result I would lose favour with the rest of the household, was to demonstrate a piety approximate to her own.

The Reverend Ponsonby came to Thirleby Hall for services only on Sundays; evening prayers were normally conducted in the house by Mrs Minim. I began to sound out my responses loud and clear, knowing that my enthusiasm would be readily apparent; and indeed it was not long before I found Mrs Minim's eyes fixed upon me with approval. And then one evening, when Mrs Minim concluded her long intercession with the Almighty, I continued to kneel, my hands clasped, my head well bent.

Betsey said, "Come on, Hattie," and gave me a vigorous prod with her foot. At which I came to with an exaggerated start. "Don't disturb me, Betsey," I said; and bent my head again.

With a mutter of contempt Betsey gave me a far from good-tempered shove; but it was as I had hoped, and Mrs Minim's eyes were upon us. "Let the child be," she commanded. After a moment or two I opened my eyes and looked round at the servants. "I was asking the Lord Jesus to forgive me for all my sins," I explained.

Betsey sniggered openly and Mrs Duckham stared, her mouth agape; but for an ally I had on one side of me a kitchen maid younger than myself who had not long left her home to come to the Hall. Much impressed by my confession, she bent her head and burst into the sobs which were never far away.

Mrs Minim came rustling forward. Her face, in the ordinary way, was set in lines as rigid as those of Mr Ogilvy's painted ancestors; but as I looked up at her with as sanctified an expression as I could command, so, miracle of miracles, I saw those lines breaking into the semblance of a smile.

"Ah," she said. "I see that after all we have here the makings of a good child. The Lord bestows His blessings where He wills."

A seed had been sown. I took to singing hymn tunes as I went about my work and with especial vigour whenever I knew Mrs Minim to be within earshot. "Who sweeps a room as for Thy laws makes that and th'action fine" I trilled, scrubbing the kitchen flagstones. It was a long time since I had shown what I was made of by kicking or biting anyone, but until this time I had nevertheless continued to regard my face and its expressions as my own property and I had continued to scowl and look morose as often as I wished to do, which was almost all the time. Now my scowls, my frowns became a thing of the past; I smiled constantly and while anyone could see me I pulled none of my old faces.

At first Mrs Duckham did not notice and I was forced to make my changed behaviour more apparent. One of her best dishes was bread and butter pudding, which she made with an abundance of eggs, cream and candied peel; the next time it was offered to us at dinner I gave my portion to Dora, the youngest kitchen maid, whose hunger was such that she could never fill her belly.

"What's this?" asked Betsey in amazement, she being the overseer of us younger ones at the bottom of the table.

"What's going on down there?" asked Mrs Duckham, expecting trouble and more than ready to sort it out with a few well-aimed blows.

"It's Harriet," said Betsey. "She's given her pudding to Dora."

"Is the child not well?" asked Mrs Duckham.

"Mrs Duckham," I replied. "It is more blessed to give than to receive."

"Is it, indeed?" said the lady. "Then that's the last pudding you'll receive in this house."

I cursed her inwardly, smiling sweetly the while, and wondering if I would ever be able to convince her of my changed self. In the weeks that followed I cursed her more and more for she and Betsey between them decided to test my new faith in every plaguing way that they could think of. I was given more work than any other of the maids and the most unpleasant tasks that either Betsey or Mrs Duckham could devise.

I could not have had a more persuasive introduction to the necessity for belief in the afterlife. For while I was ready to accept drudgery and toil far beyond my ordinary lot, that was what I was given. My reward in heaven would indeed have to be great to compensate, thought I.

Fortunately, before my patience had quite given out, Mrs Minim showed herself much impressed by my piety. Enjoying as she did a good deal more leisure and a more cultivated existence than Mrs Duckham, she was in a position in which it was easier to believe in the possibility of grace. She therefore came to believe quite rapidly that the Lord had indeed given me His special blessing and for this reason she decided that I should be relieved of some, at least, of my kitchen duties so that I could wait upon her at table.

"Harriet? Wait at table?" exclaimed Mrs Duckham in amazement.

"It will be a training for her," said Mrs Minim.

"Huh," said Mrs Duckham, not daring to comment further though showing her scepticism in every line of her face. But Mrs Minim had made up her mind. I was to take my first steps out of the kitchen and towards that other world, the world to which I knew one day I would belong.

Chapter Ten

IN GAINING Mrs Minim's favour I had taken my first step towards reaching the front of the house. It might be my fate to reach it as a maidservant, but I felt sure that I would eventually arrive there and I knew that this as Mrs Duckham's scullery help, albeit the one who knew best how to shine the copper pans, I would never do.

Now that I was near to becoming a parlour maid I was given two new cotton frocks and a new set of caps and aprons. At first I was inspected by Mrs Minim every day and several times sent away to tidy my hair or to give my work-reddened hands another wash. In those days Mrs Minim took her meals in the company of the elderly butler, Mr Fosdyke, who had been in the service of Mr Ogilvy's father and was at the last good for little except eating and drinking; so that I had to run the gauntlet not only of Mrs Minim's sharp eyes but of Mr Fosdyke's doddery gaze as well, and Mr Fosdyke did not like young girls. While Mrs Minim questioned my neatness and cleanliness, Mr Fosdyke doubted my intelligence; and yet between the two of them I learned how to wait at table in a discreet and genteel manner, all of which knowledge I instantly converted in my mind to an understanding of how, as a lady, I should expect to be waited on and what I should demand from my attendants.

Yet these ideas had to be closely concealed from my mentors; if they had suspected that I entertained such notions I would have been sent back to the scullery at once. For they believed as fervently as did the Reverend Ponsonby that each of us held here on earth a place ordained by the will of the Almighty and to question that place was to question the Almighty Himself. This was a belief held equally by Betsey, Dora and Mrs Duckham in the kitchen who obtained much less advantage from it; I could not explain even to myself why I did not accept such a belief; perhaps because as a young child, subject each week to the teachings of Mr Ponsonby, I had been withdrawn into some cave of my inner being, deaf to any instruction wise or not; and too, when I thought about it, I remembered the kindness of Mr Ogilvy who had himself come to the kitchen with that whitehaired kitten which I was sure any lady's child would have been glad to possess.

Progress I was certainly making; but so far I could not say that it had been considerable. Mrs Minim could certainly read but she appeared to do so very seldom; as far as I could tell she owned only two books, the Holy Bible and a book of devotions. I noticed that when she was reading either she did so frowningly, her brows knotted, her lips moving. "Oh, ma'am," I said to her one day. "If only I could read." But my remark provoked only a look of astonishment, not as I had hoped enthusiasm.

I thought over my ideas on the matter and recalled that it had at first occurred to me that the Reverend Ponsonby might be my instructor. He surely must be a person of greater learning than Mrs Minim and perhaps too of greater leisure. But the difficulty of how to approach him remained, a difficulty that for the moment I saw no way of solving.

And then one afternoon the opportunity came. Harry was to go into Swithindale and I was told to go with him bearing two messages; one for the dressmaker and the other for Mr Ponsonby.

In all the years I had been at Thirleby Hall I had not been far from the grounds. I sat beside Harry on the box with a shawl wrapped round me and behind us the great mansion which was Thirleby Hall dropped into the distance. I felt the fresh air on my cheeks and looked around me at the open fields rising steeply away; and I realized anew that the world of the Hall in which I lived was not the whole world as normally it seemed; but I felt so far most ill equipped to deal with it. All I knew of the outside world was that Mr Ogilvy regularly travelled in it; he spent his time in London and in Italy and in Yorkshire almost equally but I knew nothing of any of these places except the names.

"Is London near Swithindale?" I asked Harry eventually.

He laughed. "Oh no, it's a fair step from Swithindale," he said.

"A fair step." I meditated on this. "And Italy?" I asked at last. "Is that far?"

"Italy?" he pondered. "Oh, Italy," he said at last, "is very far."

Useless to question him further, I thought; for he clearly knew little more than I did myself; and my heart sank with misgivings. How, as a parlour maid, was I ever to acquire the understanding of a lady? But I was determined to try.

We came into a narrow lane which led to the village green. I had never seen so many houses grouped together. "Is London bigger than this?" I asked Harry.

"Oh ay," he replied. "You couldn't imagine London, seeing this."

"Then it must be big indeed," I said.

Harry put me down from the trap, pointing with his whip to the dressmaker's house on the green. "And where's the Rectory?" I demanded.

"Beside the church," he replied and I saw, behind the houses, a small, squat tower.

I went along to the dressmaker's house. What a noisy confusion of a place was Swithindale, I thought to myself, as I passed the little shops, heard doorbells ringing, bursts of conversation; and for a moment my heart failed me once more. What was I daring to do? At Thirleby Hall with Betsey, Mrs Duckham and Dora for companions it was not difficult for me to feel clever and brave, even intrepid. But here in the village I felt timid and afraid. And yet, I thought to myself, if I did not do something for myself, no one else would. Mr Ogilvy had taken me and given me a home; and very often I was reminded that I was fortunate to have a home; but in return for it I had to live a life of servitude.

I came to the dressmaker's house, tidy and neat with a well scrubbed front step and a shining door knocker.

When the door opened, I saw before me a diminutive maid in cap and apron who promptly at the sight of me dropped a curtsey.

How delightful that was to see! I handed her Mrs Minim's note. "From Mrs Minim at the Hall," I said in my haughtiest tone. "I am not to wait for an answer."

"No, ma'am," said the silly creature, and dropped another curtsey.

I turned away, my nose well up in the air, to effect my second errand.

The Rectory was a big square house with a plot of grass lying before it which contained only a monkey puzzle tree for ornament. As instructed by Mrs Minim, I made my way round the side of the house to the back and there knocked upon the kitchen door.

It was a cold day in autumn; the wind blew chill as I waited and I drew my shawl around me. My heart was beating fast and I was full of doubts; but I was determined nonetheless to put my request to the august reverend gentleman.

No one had answered my knock and bending my head towards the door I realized why this must be so, for there was already a considerable volume of noise coming from behind it. So I knocked again, this time more boldly; and this time the door opened.

A boy was standing there, only slightly older than myself. But this boy bore little resemblance to the ill-nourished stable lads I knew at Thirleby Hall. He was tall and slender, with golden brown hair and eyes of bright blue; but what made him most different was the welcoming smile he wore upon his face. "Come in," he commanded. "Do you wish to see my mother?"

I went over the step and into the kitchen—a kitchen such as there was at Thirleby Hall, where food was baked. But it was little like in any other respect, for behind a large deal table on which there was a profusion of dough and flour and dishes, such as Mrs Duckham would never have tolerated, stood Mrs Ponsonby removing with floury hands a long strand of hair which lay against her cheek.

If her son resembled a cherub, here I found my angel in the kindly gaze of Mrs Ponsonby. She did not bother to inquire who I was, or what my business was; she simply saw that I was cold and drew me in beside the fire.

"Please ma'am," I said. "I'm from the Hall—with a message for the Reverend Ponsonby." I was proud of the way I said that. I had practised the phrase several times over. But still I wondered if I had said it quite right for behind me I heard a titter and the smile of Mrs Ponsonby changed just a little. She took the note and gave it to the boy who had opened the door to me. "Take this to your father, Patrick," she said.

My hands out to the fire I gazed round the room. I thought I had never seen such confusion or such warmth. There were six children in the room, including a baby in a crib in one corner and also including a girl about my own age. She, like Patrick, had golden brown hair but I minded that less than the fact that she was so busily bent over the book in her lap that she had not even looked up at my entrance.

I forgot myself completely and pointed a finger at her as Mrs Minim had many times reprimanded me for doing. "Oh, ma'am," I breathed. "If only I could read like her."

Chapter Eleven

EVEN THOUGH I was by now growing up, almost a parlour maid, I still enjoyed romping in the open air and from time to time I still went off into the woods behind the house, clambering over the soft earth between the trees and up the side of the valley. There were clumps of primroses, and wild daffodils as small and shy as snowdrops; as well as these there were the birds building their nests, the rabbits hopping through the wood. I would lie down under the trees and look upwards towards the arches of the branches, sprinkled with green, and I would rub the damp earth between my fingers. And I would feel that I too had been born to live outside with the wild creatures.

But then came an afternoon when I stayed out longer than I should have done, coming back into the kitchen, tired, hungry and very dirty.

I was greeted by a resounding clout from Mrs Duckham. "And where have you been, I should like to know?" At that moment I was my old self again and I scowled at her, dodging back behind the table. She had been baking, the kitchen was very hot and so, evidently, was she; about me I still had the fresh coolness of the woods and for a moment I longed to be in the woods again. I thought of running back out of the kitchen, away from clatter and noise, raucous voices and the demands of Mrs Duckham; but I knew I would not go, for I knew now that I needed the warmth and the shelter that Thirleby Hall provided.

Mrs Duckham, arms akimbo, was still glaring at me. She said, "You'd better wash yourself, you little good for nothing. Mrs Minim wants to see you and the Reverend's with her."

The Reverend! I was reminded in an instant of the role of piety I had assumed. Hastily I stopped scowling. "Yes, Mrs Duckham," I said submissively. Behind her I saw Dora staring at me, her eyes puzzled. But Mrs Duckham herself had noticed nothing. "And be quick about it," she said and banged the rolling pin down on the table to emphasize her point.

Mrs Minim and the Reverend Ponsonby were sitting together at a little round table in Mrs Minim's parlour. Between them on the table was a decanter of wine, glasses and some of the fine biscuits which we in the kitchen were not allowed to eat. I bobbed a curtsey in the doorway.

"Come in, Harriet," said Mrs Minim.

I went quietly into the room, my eyes downcast. I wondered for a moment whether I would be reprimanded for speaking to Mrs Ponsonby of my desire to acquire an education; Mrs Ponsonby herself had seemed interested rather than shocked by my request, but I did not feel it likely that Mrs Minim would share her feeling.

And I was right. Mrs Minim was not pleased; she was not pleased at all. Her brows were drawn together in a way that I had seen previously only when Mrs Duckham had had the misfortune to serve up a burnt caramel custard. "Explain yourself, Harriet," she commanded. "What have you been saying in the village?"

"Nothing, ma'am," I said.

"Nothing indeed. I hear differently—I hear very differently. The Reverend Ponsonby tells me that you have had the impudence to approach his wife—for reading lessons. And why, may I ask, should you wish to read?"

Her face, white and furrowed, was terrifying but as I swallowed, searching for a suitable reply, I saw that beside her the Reverend Ponsonby was looking considerably less disturbed; and to my surprise he suddenly interrupted.

"If I may, Mrs Minim," he said. "I have raised this matter at Mrs Ponsonby's suggestion—"

He had given me a moment to think and in that moment I had recollected a phrase from one of his own sermons. "Please ma'am," I said, "I wants to improve my mind."

"Want," corrected the Reverend Ponsonby. "Want."

"Yes, sir," I said. "And to do that I have to read."

Mrs Minim was looking at us now with equal coldness. "And what will you improve your mind for?" she inquired at last.

Once again the Reverend Ponsonby saved me. "I hardly think," he said gently, "that that is the right question to ask. I find Harriet's suggestion wholly admirable and since my wife is prepared to undertake the task—"

"What?" At that my face burst into the biggest grin I had ever felt upon it. I could scarcely believe what I had heard.

"Oh, Mrs Minim," I cried, "please let me, please. I promise, I promise that when I can read, I will read only the Good Book."

Mrs Minim stared at me. It was clear that she did not know what to make of this enthusiasm. She looked dubiously towards the Reverend Ponsonby who was sighing and at the same time reaching towards his crystal glass of wine.

"Laudable," he said. "Most laudable."

I did not know what the word "laudable" meant, nor, I suspect, did Mrs Minim. But that he approved was evident. Mrs Minim hesitated, the remains of a frown still hovering about her face. She began, "It hardly seems . . ."

"Mrs Minim," said the Reverend Ponsonby, "you have told me yourself that you have already chosen this young person for some preferment. I confess that I cannot see any harm in her learning to read, if she wishes to do so and as long as her studies do not take her away from her tasks."

"Exactly," said Mrs Minim, triumphant. "There is more here than meets the eye. Mr Ogilvy must be consulted and there is no question of sending the trap on any special trips to Swithindale."

My face clouded. How was it possible—if, as seemed clear, Mrs Minim was against it and the approval of Mr Ogilvy himself had to be won?

"And when does Mr Ogilvy return?" asked the Reverend Ponsonby.

"Not for three weeks," said Mrs Minim. "And then you can be sure that there will be other things on his mind."

"Well, then, Harriet," said the Reverend Ponsonby. "There is your answer. You must wait for three weeks. But I conjecture that you have already waited a good deal longer."

He was right, of course; but still those three weeks seemed

extremely long. In the meanwhile I redoubled my efforts to please Mrs Minim and from time to time I did earn her praise. But as to reading, "I don't know, Harriet," she would say. "I don't know. The Lord has seen fit to call you to a place in life where you don't need to read. What would it be for?"

But then one evening, in characteristic tumult, Mr Ogilvy arrived at the Hall; and one day soon after, in response to my many reminders, Mrs Minim conducted me into the library to see him.

As I had changed with the years, so had Mr Ogilvy. He no longer appeared the huge and overbearing figure I remembered from my earlier childhood; I had grown taller and he, I fancy, was showing the passing of the years for his hair, once a shiny black, was now a good deal duller and there were more lines on his face than I remembered. In daylight the magnificent library where we found him looked even bigger than I remembered and grander. And now I noticed the books which lined the walls and I longed to know at least some of their secrets.

I stood a discreet step behind Mrs Minim as she explained my request.

"A kitchen maid," said Mr Ogilvy, "learning to read?"

I hastened to explain as best I could. "Please sir," I said, "I'm not a kitchen maid now, I wait at table."

"It's Harriet Dark, isn't it?" he said. "I remember you."

I blushed with pleasure. "Yes, sir," I said.

"Yes, I do remember. I gave you a kitten."

My whitehaired, blue-eyed kitten.

"It died, sir," I said.

"Ah," he said. "They mostly do. Which is just as well, or we'd be overrun by the creatures. Well, now, Harriet. Once you wished to run away from here. Are you happier now?"

"Oh yes, sir," I said. "As long as I can learn to read. It was you, sir, you first told me about books."

"Did I?" he said, with a faint air of being surprised at himself. "Indeed. That I do not remember. But certainly I can see no reason why you should not learn to read, if you wish to do so. And since Mrs Ponsonby is ready to teach you . . ."

"But, sir," said Mrs Minim. "How is she to get there?"

"Why, in the trap, of course," he said. "While I am away, the beasts need the exercise."

"Yes, sir," said Mrs Minim.

As far as she was concerned that was by no means the end

of it. She marched me back to the housekeeper's room and gave me a lecture on the necessity of knowing my place and not trying to get above myself. And as for Mrs Duckham, when she heard the news, she threw her apron over her head and had to be restored with several glasses of the best port. And all the time of course I had to keep my eyes demurely downcast for had anyone, anyone at all, the least idea that within the quiet creature I appeared to be there continued to live the old Harriet Dark—why there indeed there would have been an end to it, to all of it.

Chapter Twelve

But in fact that was the beginning. The beginning of my education. Twice a week I was taken by Harry in the trap to the Rectory at Swithindale, there to join in the lessons of the young Ponsonbys.

There were six Ponsonby children. The oldest was Patrick, then thirteen, and the next was Maria, eleven. Then followed Henrietta, Emily, Charlotte and the baby, who was known only as Baby and who, I gathered, would be granted the privilege of a name only when another baby had arrived to supplant him.

From the first I was in considerable awe of both Patrick and Maria. Not only were they beautiful, and their beauty made me all the more conscious of my own dark skin and tangled curls, but they were also, it was evident, very clever. As well as English—and I learned with surprise that English was a language which, without any tuition at all I had learned to speak—they could also read Latin and Greek. These, I was told, were other, older and more difficult languages. I did not aspire either to read or to speak Latin and Greek but the fact that Maria and Patrick could read them impressed me greatly.

I had to begin by reconciling myself to the fact that Charlotte at the age of four had already begun to read. When we sat together before a book it was usually she who said the word first. Mrs Ponsonby was patience itself; but the other children were not so patient.

One afternoon, on only my third or fourth visit to the Rectory, we were sitting before the fire, I with my customary primer. Mrs Ponsonby was baking, as she so often was; she knew the primer by heart and had no need to see it to correct my poor efforts. I sat dolefully struggling over the unfamiliar symbols. When I had said so blithely that I wished to learn to read, I had had no idea at all of how difficult it would be. I sat in tongue-tied silence, trying to discover what I should say. And then I leapt to my feet and went to throw the hated book on the fire.

There was a scream from Charlotte. Astonished, Mrs Ponsonby looked round and then reached out to hold my arm. "I will, I will," I shouted. "I hate it, I hate you all."

Mrs Ponsonby took me in her arms. At first I fought her away as hard as I could; then, as I had never done before, I felt my hatred and anger melting into love and the tears burst from my eyes.

All the children gathered round. "What a big girl to be crying," remarked the erudite Charlotte, and was promptly silenced by Maria. And then we were all sat at the table and given milk to drink and a small slice of plum cake to eat. After this I had fresh heart to return to the hated primer. But, sighing, Mrs Ponsonby shook her head. "I think, Harriet, we must find another way," she said.

"I have an idea, mama," said Maria. "You should give Harriet a storybook, not a baby book like Charlotte's—for she is not a baby."

Charlotte immediately sent up a scream that she was not a baby either. But Mrs Ponsonby gave due consideration to Maria's idea. That the Ponsonby children were allowed to speak thus to their parents was a continual amazement to me. "I think you are right, Maria," said Mrs Ponsonby after some thought. "All of you were fortunate enough to begin to read when you were very small; Harriet is older and the same book is not suitable for her."

"She knows her letters by now, does she not, mama? Then I think, if we give her an interesting story to read, she will find out a good deal for herself."

She went at once to her room, fetched one of her own books and began reading it to me. I had never been so enthralled in my life; but then I heard the knock on the back door of Harry the groom come to fetch me. "Here, Harriet," said Maria. "Take it—and see if you can begin to read the rest for yourself."

I sat behind Harry on the ride back to Thirleby Hall and

studied the first page of the story of Cinderella. By the time we reached the Hall and, my stomach queasy, I climbed down from the cart, the miracle had been accomplished. The sounds I spoke with my mouth and the symbols I saw on the page had come together. Haltingly, very haltingly, I could read. Laughing I ran into the kitchen and pulling little Dora away from the sink I danced round the room with her.

"What's this, what's this?" asked Mrs Duckham.

"I can read, Mrs Duckham, I can read," I shouted.

"Eh, happen next you'll be marrying Mr Ogilvy," she snorted. With the tale of Cinderella fresh in my mind, I stopped abruptly in my dance and stared at her. "Yes," I said. "Maybe I will."

Mrs Duckham's mocking words had awakened something in my mind, a fantasy which on being named came forward out of a dark recess which I myself had not been aware of. I found that night after night the same figure appeared in my dreams; the dreams were not always the same but they were dominated by a tall figure of a man in riding cloak and boots, whose face I could never see. I thought that so Mr Ogilvy might have first appeared to me when I was a very small child.

The dreams both frightened and excited me. Sometimes the tall figure was a long way off and I would be running towards it; sometimes it was confronting me and I was retreating from it in terror. Marry Mr Ogilvy? I did not know—but I could not conceive of marrying anyone else.

At times this strange land of my dreams, of pursuit, of almost-capture, seemed more real than my everyday life, fed as it was by the storybooks which, now that I could read, I brought back with me from Swithindale. This was hardly surprising considering the monotonous routine of the life that I led as a parlour maid, cleaning endlessly, polishing, waiting at table; small wonder that my thoughts would stray into daydreams.

The afternoons when I went to Swithindale to the Rectory were quite different; then I had no difficulty in keeping my mind upon what I was doing as, "For heaven's sake, has the child no gumption?" I was urged twenty times a day by Mrs Duckham. Mrs Ponsonby had been a governess before her marriage and for that reason, I believe, was counted something less than a lady by the undisputed holders of that title in the neighbourhood; but she was most certainly a lady in the gentle, pious nature she displayed, and the afternoons I spent in her company were the happiest I had ever known.

My devotion to her was very great. I would silence the younger children for her, I would collect up the books for her, I would bring her bunches of wild flowers. "I believe Harriet loves you as much as we do, mama," said Maria one day. More, I said to myself; but not aloud.

And through my devotion I learned a great deal from her, and not only in reading and writing. Mrs Ponsonby's voice was quiet; I learned to moderate mine. Mrs Ponsonby did not wipe her nose on her sleeve, Mrs Ponsonby did not belch. These were old habits of mine which, following Mrs Ponsonby's example, I did my best to discard.

I did not feel as much at home with Patrick and Maria as I did with their mother; for as I had been from the first I continued to be timid in their company. I did not care to admit this; were they not children, just like myself? But they were not just like myself; I felt a difference between us, not only in our manners, but in our inner selves. They were beautiful, as anyone could see and as I was not. But what was more important was that while for months before I had been deliberately cultivating piety with scant results except on the surface, Maria and Patrick seemed to me to be genuinely good.

Each afternoon we were turned out of doors into the Rectory garden for half an hour's exercize. The first time this happened I stood hesitantly by the door, looking up at the church tower which overshadowed the garden and across at the leaning tombstones. To the best of my recollection, I had never played in a garden before; at Thirleby Hall gardens were places where precious things were grown and there was no wild running about in them. I was used to running wild only in the woods, in truly wild places. But, "Come on, Harriet," said Maria and pulled me into a game of tig.

I soon understood what the game was about. My way of catching someone, when I began to play, was simply to knock them to the ground and to sit on them, and my first choice of a victim was Patrick.

He looked up at me in astonishment. Maria said, "Harriet, let him get up." Reluctantly, I moved over. "I say," said Patrick, "you do play rough." When Mrs Ponsonby called us in, she reprimanded Patrick severely for the state of his jacket and I waited to hear him tell her that it was all my fault. What would my punishment be, I wondered? Would they send me away? Say that I must never come to Swithindale again?

But Patrick said only, "Sorry, mama," and the others said not a word. When Mrs Ponsonby turned away, he looked at me and winked. I gazed back at him in amazement. From the first I had felt that Maria and Patrick were of a different race from myself; now I was sure of it.

As I remember now, the rides back to Thirleby Hall were always conducted in the gray and melancholy light of gathering dusk. How I hated to be going away from the Rectory instead of towards it, how I wished that my true place was there, where I felt it to be, with Mrs Ponsonby and the others. Now and then Mrs Ponsonby would tuck into my pocket a piece of oatcake to eat on the journey; I would finger this and one by one slip small crumbs of it into my mouth; but often I could not swallow the crumbs for the sobs which were rising in my throat.

I spent much less time now in the stables with Harry the groom and in the vegetable gardens with Mr Bennett. "You're becoming quite a stranger, young lass," said Mr Bennett to me one evening. He was engaged in scraping his boots by the kitchen door, while I got down from the pony cart. "Yes, indeed," I said. "Can you not see that I have quite changed?"

He looked at me solemnly, and for a long time afterwards I remembered his words. "Changed?" he said. "You've not changed. You never have and you never will."

Chapter Thirteen

Mr Bennett remained uncertain and suspicious of my new-found refinement; not so Mrs Minim. I soon discovered that it was no longer necessary to pretend to sanctity to keep her friendship, for she appeared to be genuinely fond of me as I had become. I was much relieved to be rid of this particular pretence, for it had always sat on me most uneasily.

Now, when I was not at the Rectory, I spent more and more time in the company of Mrs Minim, becoming gradually quite indispensable to her. I ran errands and carried messages and as she went about the great rooms of the house I went with her, reminding her of what needed to be done when, as it very often happened, she had forgotten.

In her demeanour even to myself Mrs Minim remained the forbidding figure I remembered from my first encounter with her; but as, under the gentle tuition of Mrs Ponsonby, my understanding and knowledge of character increased, I came to see her as far from dragon-like and scarcely even formidable except on the surface. She was not much educated; she had reached the eminence of her position not, as I had thought, by virtue of being born almost a lady, but rather in spite of her birth, for she had begun work in the household many years before as a maid in the time of the father of the Mr Ogilvy I knew, and had become housekeeper after a long apprenticeship.

Mr Fosdyke, her old ally and companion in the household,

eventually died to the regret of no one except Mrs Minim. He was replaced by one of the much younger footmen who preferred to continue to dine with Mrs Duckham and the others in the kitchen, so that Mrs Minim's position of eminence became a lonely one indeed.

Even under the influence of Mr Fosdyke, Mrs Minim had never become a drinker and she did not do so now; but her mind began to wander in a way that might well have been attributed to excessive drinking. Now that the butler was so much younger than herself and, what was more, chose to league himself with Mrs Duckham, she began to feel increasingly uncertain of her own authority and tried to maintain it by a host of quixotic orders which were in danger of making her a laughing stock. Edward, the new butler, was continually being asked for lists of the stocks held in the wine cellar; when I presented him with the request for the second time in a fortnight, he nudged me and winked and said, with a gesture of the elbow, "What's the old girl up to then, Harriet?" I did my best to conceal Mrs Minim's condition from the rest of the household, but she allowed me no alternative but to carry out her orders.

The closeness of my relations with Mrs Minim began now to aggravate another difficulty which I had been aware of from the first. More and more I was the envy of Betsey and all the others in the kitchen, even of Dora who had once been my friend and champion. Their discontent centred itself upon my visits to Swithindale, Mrs Duckham declaring that she saw no reason why I should have better treatment than the others, rather the reverse. I was not, like the others, a girl of respectable birth, I was an abandoned child and had I not from the first shown a vile and surly disposition? It was pointed out that since then my disposition had improved. "Eh, pigs can fly,"sneered Mrs Duckham. For the first time for years she lumbered out of the kitchen quarters and into Mrs Minim's room to place before her a demand that my lessons should stop at once.

Mrs Minim's first response to this was to insist that as the lessons were taking place on her instructions they were to continue; and continue they did. But when it became clear to her that my original goal of learning to read had long since been reached, then, in Mr Ogilvy's absence she took it upon herself at last to order that the lessons be discontinued.

"Too much learning, Harriet," she said, "cannot be good."

As soon as I could contrive it, I went to the Rectory to ask

Mrs Ponsonby's help. "Please, Mrs Ponsonby," I begged, "you must do something."

To my great dismay she shook her head. "I am sorry, Harriet. If Mr Ogilvy were here, we could go to him, but as it is I think there is nothing to be done."

I burst into a fit of noisy sobs; not for me then the slow, quiet tears of a lady. "There, there," said Mrs Ponsonby. "But, Harriet, all is not lost—now at least you are equipped to go on by yourself. You can read, you can study and from time to time you will be able to come here again."

All this was true and as I wiped my eyes I tried to acknowledge that it was so but the grief that could not be assuaged was the grief of another parting from creatures whom I loved; and once again in this moment I relived the grief I had felt on leaving my mother all those years ago.

Mrs Ponsonby gave me a letter for Mrs Minim, which I held sullenly all the long silent journey home. Hating both of them for my disappointment I wanted to tear the letter up and send the pieces out to the unfeeling hills. But the sweetness of Mrs Ponsonby's voice was still in my ears; and so at last I did present her letter to Mrs Minim.

That evening I waited on Mrs Minim at dinner as usual. My eyes were red with crying, my manner deliberately ungracious. Once a terrifying and dictatorial figure, Mrs Minim was such no longer; rather she was timid and diffident and she watched me at work with growing unease. At last, a conciliatory smile on her lips, she spoke to me of Mrs Ponsonby's letter. "I am inclined to agree with Mrs Ponsonby," she said.

"Then I may go on?" I asked.

She frowned. "No, indeed, Harriet, you must not think of it. But Mrs Ponsonby suggests that in Mr Ogilvy's absence you may from time to time make use of the library. I do not think I need object to that."

I dropped the expected curtsey. "Thank you, Mrs Minim," I said; and yet my heart remained heavy. For more than the books and the learning that I had found at the Rectory, it was the friendship which I valued and that, in an empty room, I would not find. For a day or two I deliberately did not avail myself of the permission I had been given, confining myself to my usual household tasks. But then at last the boredom and monotony of that routine sent me back to the books which with Mrs Ponsonby's help I had come to love.

She had told me what a magnificent library Mr Ogilvy possessed and exploring it for myself I saw that this was indeed so. As often as I could, I went there to read, finding comfort from the dull, indifferent world of the kitchens of Thirleby Hall in the aphorisms of Dr Johnson, the poetry of Milton and Pope. I remembered Mrs Ponsonby's words: "Mr Ogilvy is a most cultivated gentleman," and I saw from his library that this must be true.

I was not quite without news of the Rectory for the Reverend Ponsonby continued to visit the chapel each Sunday. Now that he knew me he would pause even in the midst of his still hasty departures to ask how I was and to give me news of his own family. And so I learned quite soon after my departure from the Rectory that Patrick was to go away to school. Therefore, our friendship could not have continued as it had done before, I thought to myself; and this thought did console me a little.

Chapter Fourteen

NOW, MORE and more, I became the shadow of Mrs Minim and as her shadow I had entry to all the rooms at the front of Thirleby Hall. If I was found on the main staircase, it was understood that I was there on Mrs Minim's business. And while Mrs Duckham believed that I was working for Mrs Minim, and Mrs Minim knew little of the whereabouts of anyone, I spent as much time as I could in the library.

While I sat reading, I also daydreamed and I found it easier to daydream when I was not wearing a maid's cap and apron. So I arranged myself in Mr Ogilvy's own chair, reading a novel belonging to Mr Ogilvy and wearing a plain, dark dress. Anyone who saw me, I reflected, would be certain to think me a young lady for with my hair smoothed back and my prim demeanour I bore a close resemblance to Maria Ponsonby and she, as the Rector's daughter, was most certainly a young lady.

At this time Mr Ogilvy's absence from the Hall had been unusually prolonged. He had been in Italy, Mrs Minim informed me, and then instead of returning to Yorkshire as was his usual habit he had, for some reason, decided to stay in London for a while. I began to imagine that Mr Ogilvy would not now return to Thirleby Hall until he could take me as his bride; the longer he stayed away, the more contented I was, for I knew that I was growing steadily into a young woman.

And there was no reason now to stay a child; no Maria to play tig with, no cherished Mrs Ponsonby to claim as a mother.

So regularly each night and morning I brushed my hair and walked about the Hall as sedately as I knew how. It seemed to me, as I caught passing glimpses in the mirror of my pale face, my almost smooth hair, that I certainly was on the point of becoming a young lady whom Mr Ogilvy could marry.

The reality of my everyday existence was in strong contrast to this belief; I still waited at table, I still went on my knees to clean carpets and I still slept at night in a tiny attic room. But for large portions of the day I managed to contrive that I sat reading and reflecting in ladylike stillness; and so my dreams grew and prospered.

And then word was received. Mr Ogilvy was to return, and not alone. A large party was to accompany him. The whole house was set immediately into an uproar.

In the days following the receipt of this news I worked as hard as anyone. Curtains were taken down, washed and rehung, covers taken off furniture and carpets. By the day of his expected arrival, everything was ready; fires had been lit all over the house, beds made and aired. And on that day, recklessly continuing in my fantasy, I dared to sit before the great fire in the library, warming my toes, and reading *Northanger Abbey*.

I was still safe, I assured myself. The windows of the library overlooked the park and the avenue of trees which led to the house from the road. I would be certain to hear the carriages approaching and I would have plenty of time to make good my escape. Or so I thought, for I had not heard a sound when the door opened and into the room walked the tall and darkhaired figure of my dreams, Mr Ogilvy himself. And not alone, for at his side there was a young woman in riding habit her face flushed beneath a broadbrimmed hat, a most extraordinarily beautiful face.

I jumped up and curtseyed.

"What the deuce?" said Mr Ogilvy. The lady said nothing; she simply directed to me her wide and shining gaze; and my erstwhile model of beauty, Maria Ponsonby, faded for ever into insignificance.

"And who are you?"

"I am Harriet Dark, sir."

"Harriet Dark?" He repeated the words in a tone of astonishment. At least as in my dreams I had surprised him. What would he say next? Would he comment on the extraordinary refinement I had developed in his absence?

He did not. Instead, he burst out laughing. Then turning to his companion he said, "Nina—I must tell you who this child is. I found her at Steepleton Fair many years ago and now she is a maid in this house. We have done well by her, have we not?"

"Well, indeed." The pink mouth smiled.

As he had said, I was a maid in his household. And when he identified me thus, every vestige of my hard-won refinement fell away from me. Stumbling over my feet, grinning like an idiot, I ran from the room. As I ran, so I heard his laughter rising behind me.

Chapter Fifteen

"MARK MY WORDS," said Mrs Duckham. "This time he's hooked—and not before time, too. She's the Honourable Nina Sanctuary and she's a beauty. Isn't that so, Hattie?"

One round, red elbow jogged my arm. I did not answer; I had come to understand long before that, whenever she called me Hattie, it was in order to tease and her teasing was best deflected by silence.

"And is she rich too?" asked Betsey from further down the table. I looked at her disdainfully; she had the gloating expression and rounded eyes of someone listening to a fairy tale. To her, no doubt, fairy tale figures they were, Mr Ogilvy and his bride, just as once Mr Ogilvy had been to me. But already that seemed to me a long time ago for now that Mr Ogilvy had returned it was he who interested me and the figure of my dreams had disappeared. And as real was the Honourable Nina Sanctuary, chestnut curls, blue eyes and all. Might I not have been as beautiful, had I had all her advantages? Had she not come like a thief in the night to take what I desired for myself?

Mr Ogilvy had brought reality home with him. I could no longer daydream in his library, imagining myself a young lady, even a princess; now I was back where I had always been, in the kitchens and confined to my servant's life. And now I knew how much I hated it.

Mrs Duckham had paused before replying, holding before her mouth a large chunk of stewed beef. Putting it at last into her mouth she spoke through the whole mouthful. "I believe," she said, "that she is. Oh yes, she's the daughter of Lord Sanctuary and he'll have money, I'll be bound. Though he has no need of it."

"Who?" asked Betsey, momentarily confused.

"Mr Ogilvy, of course," retorted Mrs Duckham. "Mr Ogilvy has plenty—even enough for our Hattie here, I shouldn't wonder—and we all know what a big appetite she has."

There were titters at this all the way down the table. I looked down at the large plate of beef, carrots and potatoes before me and remembered the menus I had written out that morning for the dining-room. Beef there was in quantity for the ladies and gentlemen; but there were also quails, pheasant, trout. The choice was for Nina Sanctuary, not for me.

"Not eating, eh, my duck?" asked Mrs Duckham. Her mouth was open, showing the few blackened teeth she had left; I had a strong desire to hurl my mug of beer into her face and for a moment I allowed myself to picture how delightful it would be to see her coughing and spluttering, the drops running down her greasy cheeks; but I could calculate, as I had not been able to do as a child, how much such a gesture would cost me, and instead I raised the mug to my lips.

I said gravely, "Let us hope, Mrs Duckham, that the beef is tenderer than this—for the table. Otherwise, we're sure to have the master down on us."

"Eh? What?" said Mrs Duckham, distracted. "It's beautiful."

"But hardly for delicate palates," I remarked.

"O'course," sneered Mrs Duckham. "You'd be knowing about that, Hattie, wouldn't you?"

I made no reply, only continuing to eat with as much appetite as I could muster. Mrs Duckham went on shovelling in her portion but angrily now, with beetled brows.

I escaped that afternoon from the house and walked up through the woods. There was a place, a little grassy hill, which had long been a favourite of mine where the trees broke and from which it was possible to see both the house and the full stretch of parkland beyond. I had spent many an afternoon there, picturing myself as Mr Ogilvy's wife and mistress of all that I could see, and as I reached the place and sank down on to the grass my dreams came back into my mind; but how bitter they tasted now that I could see them so clearly as nothing more than dreams.

I was ten years or so younger than Nina Sanctuary and many more years younger than Mr Ogilvy. I was almost grown up, almost educated; so much I had seen to by my own efforts. And yet beside the chosen figure of Nina Sanctuary I was still, it was plain, not a woman at all but a child. If only, I thought, clasping my hands together in an agony of longing, if only Mr Ogilvy had waited—just for a few more years. It was intolerable that after so long he should decide to marry now, when it was still too soon.

I heard a rustling in the woodland above me. Someone was coming on horseback. There was the sound of a man's voice, a laugh—it was Mr Ogilvy himself. He must not find me idle again, usurping a lady's place; quickly I got up and scrambled away from the hillock on which I had been sitting to hide behind a wide, gnarled trunk.

There was a chink of bridles and the murmur of voices. It was, as I had thought, Mr Ogilvy; with him was Nina Sanctuary. Suddenly they were very near and I realized that they had got down from their horses and were leading them through the woods. I flattened myself against the tree, even more frightened now that they would find me. But a moment later they passed, walking down towards the house.

I stood staring after them, confident now that they would not look behind them. But as I watched I saw more than I bargained for, for suddenly he stopped and took her into his arms. I had seen kisses in plenty and more, but never before had I seen a man kiss a woman in that way; he clasped his arms around her and they came together as if in the union of parts of one body instead of two; and so, for several minutes, they stayed. And while they stayed thus, I watched them.

They came apart at last and moved on, his hand under her elbow. Left behind on the hill I flung myself to the ground in a passion of tears. I had seen something in that moment that I wanted even more than I wanted Mr Ogilvy himself. And I felt quite sure that it could never be mine.

That very day by mischance I was thrown into the constant company of Nina Sanctuary. Her maid had taken a fever and was confined to bed. "She has asked for you, Harriet," said Mrs Minim.

"For *me*?"

"Yes, most particularly, by name."

I thought then that she must remember our encounter in the

library. How else would she know my name? "But I'm no lady's maid," I said.

"You're to go up just the same. Her ladyship's maid will dress her hair—you will be there to help."

I thought for a moment of rebelling; it gave me a strange pain to think of being so close to the object of Mr Ogilvy's love. But then I thought how much I might learn of that exotic creature, a lady as Mrs Ponsonby was a lady, but how different. So meekly I said, "Yes, Mrs Minim," and went upstairs.

Chapter Sixteen

ON MR OGILVY'S explicit instructions the Honourable Nina Sanctuary had been given one of the most beautiful rooms in the house. Decorated in yellow and white, it contained a large fourposter bed which, standing on a little dais, was hung with pale yellow curtains. I myself had helped to make up the bed with clean linen, smelling of herbs from the closet; I wished now I had strewn it with nettles. But to perpetrate even such a trick as that would not have driven the blackness from my heart, or so I thought as I paused before the door, feeling sure that so much hatred must show itself upon my face however hard I tried to hide it. I must keep my eyes lowered, I thought; or it surely will show.

Resolving at all costs to go unnoticed, I tapped gently at the door and heard a summons to enter. I duly went in.

She was sitting on a small white carved chair before the looking glass, her hair hanging down her back. "Come in, come in," she said, as hesitantly I stood by the door.

I was no more used to her beauty now than I had been the first time I had seen her. Her hair, very long and thick, was a truly extraordinary colour like the turned leaves of autumn, copper-red but glinting yellow when the candle light caught it in its flickering beams. Against her hair her skin was an unearthly white. She was wearing a pale, loose robe and I could almost have thought that a figure had come to life and stepped down from one of the huge paintings in the hall, in which angels and archangels frolicked and swam in blue celestial air.

She looked at me as I looked at her and I suppose I must have shown in my face not my hatred and envy of her for, in my dreams, supplanting me, but rather my homage to her beauty. And she smiled and our eyes held together. But then I became aware of something in her face which I had not seen before; there was a meanness in that splendid face, a smugness and a cruelty which boded ill for Mr Ogilvy or anyone else who remained close to her; it lay in the flared nose, in the quick tuck of the lips; and then, as if she had seen my expression change according to my perception, so, abruptly, she looked away. I lowered my eyes and she turned back to the glass without speaking.

I did not have to be told what was to be done. There were clothes strewn all over the room, the riding clothes she had discarded in one corner, the cupboard doors open as if she had been rifling through all her wardrobe. I began picking things up, setting aside what needed to be washed or pressed. Her boots were caked with mud; I picked them up and looked at them, smelling once again the fresh earth of the woods that I loved even in this warm and perfumed room.

"You, you, what's your name?"

I realized that someone was speaking to me. There were three women in the room besides myself, the maid, Nina Sanctuary and an older lady whom I guessed to be her mother. It was she who had called out to me.

I curtseyed. "Harriet, ma'am."

"Well, Harriet, ring the bell, will you?"

The bellknob was in the wall within reach of her hand. I crossed the room and pulled it.

If Nina Sanctuary was remarkable for her beauty, her mother was not less so for her ugliness. Surely the sight of her was enough to make Mr Ogilvy think again? For they were alike but in a grotesque fashion; where Nina was plump, her mother was gross, the fair skin of the young woman was broken by veins in the older one and even the glorious hair looked harsh against the older face. But more than that, the meanness I had glimpsed in Nina's face was written very large upon her mother's. What life had such a face passed through, I wondered, and thought that this was something I would not learn from all the books in Mr Ogilvy's library.

One of the maids entered in response to the bell.

"Bring some refreshment, will you?" said Lady Sanctuary. "A little claret, some sandwiches."

"Yes, ma'am," said the girl, bobbing. It was less than an hour before dinner and a sumptuous dinner at that, as I knew well. "How I *loathe* the country. It gives one an appetite and *nothing* to do with it," said Lady Sanctuary and gave an enormous yawn.

My tidying done, I came to stand by the dressing-table. The hair of the Honourable Nina Sanctuary had to be dressed three times with three completely different sets of jewelled combs before she was satisfied, and I was glad indeed that the task was not mine. The choosing of a gown took even longer but at last she decided upon a white gown trimmed with gold embroidery, floating wide upon an enormous collection of petticoats.

"Lovely, my dear," said her mother. "It reminds me of the night—I was scarcely seventeen—when Prinny and I . . . "

But Nina turned aside, making no pretence at listening, and her mother fell silent. I felt a moment's pity for her; time had transmuted her beauty so completely into ugliness, and the perfection of her daughter emphasized the fact. And then I saw her raising a satisfied hand to her hair and I realized that what I saw as the ruin of her beauty might appear very differently to her.

As the two ladies descended the stairs to dinner the maid and I put the room into order. Lady Sanctuary's woman was neat and wizened; there could scarcely have been a greater contrast between herself and the lady whom she served. I looked into the glass at my own face, the bushy brown hair, thick eyebrows, straight nose, and I wondered whether in thirty years' time mine would be the thin face of someone who had given her life in service. And with a pang of fear I knew that if I stayed at Thirleby Hall in my present condition I could expect no other fate. I made up my mind that come what may I would not accept it.

Chapter Seventeen

FOR THE PRESENT there was nothing else I could do. And what was worse, as long as Mr Ogilvy and his guests were in the house, I could not pretend to be anything other than a housemaid. The library was now closed to me, all the state rooms of the house were out of bounds except when I was carrying out some menial duty. Chafe as I did against my bonds there was no alternative but to accept them.

I went sulkily about my tasks, feeling the rage growing inside me, not bothering to conceal my resentment and distaste for the obligations of the life that was mine. I did not consider in fact that there was any need to hide my feelings; certainly it did not seem likely that Mr Ogilvy and his friends would concern themselves with the emotions of a mere servant.

And then I discovered that someone did appear to have noticed my scowls, frowns, muttered grumblings. Not Mrs Minim, nor Mrs Duckham; with the household expanded as it was, both of these personages had little time to notice anything. No, it was no less a person than Nina Sanctuary herself.

Her maid had soon recovered and resumed her duties. But, Mrs Minim told me, it was the particular request of Miss Nina that I should continue my personal service to her. The order had to be accepted; with the household in such confusion my position as Mrs Minim's favourite had been virtually forgotten. But I did not do so with pleasure. While I dusted and polished I could always daydream; it was much more difficult to see myself as the bride of Mr Ogilvy when I was so much in the company of the lady who was in fact, as it now seemed, to give her hand to Mr Ogilvy in marriage.

I went about her room picking up her shoes, those extraordinarily tiny shoes into which I, still almost a child, could never have fitted my feet. I folded her shawls, put away her jewels and hated her from the bottom of my heart.

And then one evening as I worked, glowering with resentment, I caught her eye in the glass. She was leaning forward to apply a little pearl powder with her small and delicate fingers and by accident, at the same moment, my scowling face loomed up into the mirror, my eyes dark with jealousy, hers wide and apparently candid. But I had always suspected that candour, that innocence, and my suspicions were proved now to be well-founded.

We were alone in the room together at that moment. Her maid had gone downstairs, her mother too was temporarily absent. She said, "Harriet."

"Yes, ma'am."

"Come here."

"Yes, ma'am."

I went to stand next to her. As best I could I smoothed out my expression, but so great was my resentment that I felt sure that I could not quite have succeeded; and I was right, as I saw in the glass where a frown still hovered over my forehead.

"Harriet, you surprise me," said Nina. "Come, come," and she beckoned me closer. Then, wrinkling her nose, she waved me away again. "Good heavens, how you smell of the stable."

Her own person exuded a great many odours, natural and perfumed. I wanted to be close to her and to drink them in and yet at the same time I felt sure that there was a danger there. Somehow she would make me suffer.

She was looking at her own reflection and the contented smile on her face showed the pleasure she felt at what she saw. "Yes, well," she said. Then she looked at me. "But what are we going to do about you?" she asked.

I said nothing. My hands, my brown hands, were clasped in front of me and I looked down at them.

"I hear you can read," she said. "Thanks to the goodness of the household which took you in, you have been able to acquire something of an education."

"Oh yes," I said eagerly. "I can read and I know all the Kings of England—"

She burst out laughing. "Do you indeed," she said at last. "Well, I'm sure that knowledge will prove most useful to you."

I felt tears at the back of my eyes. She could afford to laugh at my attempts to better myself. To me learning offered the only escape I could think of from my predicament.

The door into the room opened. It was her maid returning. "Well, Harriet," said Nina. "As long as I am here you shall work for me, assisting Williams. When I am ready to leave, then we shall see whether you have been able to learn anything from me which will be of real use to you."

I wondered what she meant. What could I learn from her which would help me in my pursuit? It was no part of my ambition to be a lady's maid.

She put out her hand as if to pat my cheek, but the pat turned into a stinging blow made the more painful by the rings with which her hand was laden. I cried out with the pain, but already she had turned back to the mirror. "Your first lesson, Harriet," she said calmly. "I fear Mr Ogilvy has been much too generous to you—you have not yet learned to respect your betters."

There was no escaping her.

"Please, Mrs Minim," I said, "let me—" but she would not listen. "For goodness' sake, Harriet, there is so much to be done," she would say and away she would go. But much as I longed to be released from the uncertain service of Mr Ogilvy's bride, still I found myself fascinated by her so that I could think of nothing else; whenever I was in her presence I found my eyes fixed upon her, the bright hair, the white skin. I saw now that her beauty was not the only attraction she exercized, or even the most important one; she had within her an extraordinary quality of strength which appeared now as bravery, now as a most coldblooded cruelty. Mr Ogilvy dwelt about her like a man possessed; she would glide down the steps into the great hall almost as if floating upon her billowing skirts and he would go to meet her, holding out his hand to her as if he wanted nothing more than to take her completely into his being; and then again, when she was dressed for riding in a severe habit, her hair tucked beneath her hat, a riding crop in her gloved palm, she was a fearsome sight indeed. But beautiful, always beautiful.

After our first brief conversation she did not speak to me directly for several days. The blow on the face had made me apprehensive; now, in her presence, I did my best to appear merely the housemaid I was, creeping about to do my duties, keeping my eyes lowered; but as the days went on and she paid me no attention, then I soon forgot her warning and became my old self again, resentful of the duties I had to perform simply because of the station in life to which I had been born; the old scowls appeared on my face and I breathed the old sighs.

And then one evening the summons came. All that day I had worked carelessly, with reluctance, and while dusting her room I had knocked over and broken a small glass ornament which stood on her dressing-table. Hastily, hoping that she would not notice, I had bundled the pieces away and then had forgotten the incident.

Williams came into the kitchen. "She wants you, Harriet, at once," she said. "And she's in a right mood, I can tell you."

"What have you done now, Harriet?" asked Mrs Duckham.

"Done? Nothing except my work," I answered.

"Hm," snorted Mrs Duckham. "You can't trust that girl, not an inch. She comes of thieving stock, she does." But for once I scarcely heard her. I was already hurrying out of the kitchen and up the back stairs. For, as I now discovered, fear of what she might do was mingled in almost equal parts with an excitement which I did not clearly understand. I knew that fierce though she was and cruel though she could be, she was also more beautiful than any other creature I had ever seen. How soft her skin was, how gentle her touch could be, if she should allow it.

"Ah, Harriet," she said, as I came into the room. I stood at the door, feeling a chill apprehension in the pit of my stomach. And yet I knew there was also a silly, eager smile on my face.

"Yes, ma'am," I said, and bobbed a curtsey.

She stood looking at me. She was wearing her white robe and her hair was loose. Dressed in this manner she had always the appearance of belonging to some other world, a world which I could never enter, a world at whose spirituality I could only guess. But her voice, when it came, seemed to bite into my skin.

"There is something missing, Harriet," she said. "From my table."

The ornament! At the time the incident had not seemed to me to have the least importance and I had forgotten all about it. I said, "Missing, ma'am?"

She gave a "tch" of impatience. "So we have here a liar as well as a thief."

"Oh, not a thief, ma'am," I said. "I didn't steal it, it fell."

"So you do know what I'm talking about?"

I hung my head.

"I see," she said. "Well, you're evidently a clever child, but not quite clever enough."

"I didn't mean—"

"You will not argue with me. Do you hear?"

I looked down at my feet. In my longing to flee they were twisted round each other. I was still by the door and in one way it would have been easy, but I knew that to run away would only be to increase my punishment.

"Now, clever child," she said, and again her voice stung me. "Shall we turn you over to the constables?"

"Oh no, ma'am."

"I don't see why not. A stay in prison would surely teach you better ways."

Prison! Tears sprang into my eyes at the thought. Not even my mother had suffered that disgrace, as far as I knew. If I went to prison I might never be taken in anywhere again. "Oh, please ma'am," I said. "I didn't steal it, on my honour I didn't."

"On your honour," she repeated. Every word I used seemed only to incite her sarcasm. "And what would the honour of a housemaid be, I wonder? I'm certain you were dishonoured long ago."

I pressed my hand against my eyes in a vain effort to stop the tears flowing. "Please, ma'am," I said again.

"Oh very well," she said, in a bored kind of voice. "But if you are to escape what should be your punishment, then I must punish you myself."

"Oh thank you, ma'am," I said.

"Thank you?" she repeated. "I wonder if you will thank me when I have finished. Take off your clothes, Harriet."

"My clothes, ma'am?"

"Your clothes."

As I continued to gape at her, she turned away. She was going to beat me, it was clear, and I had had enough beatings already in my life for a beating of itself to hold fear for me. But all my clothes? Slowly I began to do as I was told, dropping my cap, apron, dress and shift in a heap upon the floor.

She did not look round and I knew better than to draw

attention to myself. I simply waited, naked and shivering. At last she said,"What a poor little animal it is." But the tone of her voice belied her words.

"Lie down," she said, and nodded her head towards the chaise longue which stood before the fire.

I ran across to it and did as I was told, burying my head in one of the cushions. The next moment she pulled it away from me with a curse and my chin jolted against the upholstery. "Turn over," she said.

I lay quite flat looking at her. She was holding her riding crop and I knew then that the punishment I would suffer at her hands would be worse than any other. But she was taking her time before she began, staring down at my body.

"What is that?" she asked at last, pointing to the scar on my arm.

"It's where I was bitten once—by a rat."

She said, "Ugh! Disgusting—" Then, in a kind of swift reaction to the horror my body awoke in her, she brought the stick down.

I endured it, my punishment, without crying out and it did not last long. She contented herself with only a handful of the most savage blows she could inflict; and then she dropped the stick. "You are a contemptible creature, Harriet," she announced. "If you wish, you may tell your Mrs Minim that you have committed a very grave misdemeanour and that you have been punished for it."

I spent that night lying on my bed. I kept on my clothes over my wounds and my eyes stayed shocked and open. But no light came, there was no light either within my soul or without.

Chapter Eighteen

THE NEXT afternoon I left the house and made my way up to the ridge; and there I climbed a tree as I had been used to do as a small child and sat on one of the branches looking out over the vale of Swithindale. Below me was the house where I had spent all the life that I could remember; and beyond it the great park stretched into the distance until the farmland began. It was large, splendid and magnificent, as magnificent in its appearance as Nina Sanctuary was in hers, and I was permitted a lodging there; but I lodged like a bird under the eaves; only a tiny place was mine and that might be taken from me at any time.

And then, looking beyond the park to the village of Swithindale in the distance I thought of the Rectory and of the Ponsonbys. But though I longed with all my heart for the comfort Mrs Ponsonby could give me, I did not plan to go to her; I had been punished, savagely punished, but punished nonetheless for a wrongdoing; Mrs Ponsonby would not have treated me in such a way but Mrs Ponsonby would still have acknowledged that I had done wrong. Maria, Patrick, all those at the Rectory whom I loved seemed now to be an extraordinary distance away; and I could feel only my tormentors near at hand.

As it grew dusk, I climbed down from my tree and walked back to the house.

"She wants you, and be quick about it," snapped Mrs Duckham. "She's got your measure and no mistake."

I went up the back stairs to the yellow and white bedroom. Whatever awaited me there I knew I could not escape it.

"Ah, Harriet," she said as I entered. She was sitting before her dressing table, tapping her fingers; and involuntarily I shuddered. She laughed. "Fetch me my robe, will you, Harriet?" she said.

In the house the merrymaking continued. At last I was seeing for myself the lives true ladies led, and marvelling at them. Every evening after dinner there was music, games, dancing, while in the daytime the ladies read, or embroidered, or strolled about the park, or rode out on horseback, sustaining themselves through this activity by a quite amazing quantity of food and wine. Lady Sanctuary, as was common talk among the servants, drank more wine and brandy than old Mr Fosdyke had done; the only difference was that, unlike the old butler, she gave no appearance of being affected by it.

I crept in and out of this glittering company like a mouse. I had no thought now but of avoiding punishment.

And then one day I encountered Mr Ogilvy. It was a momentary encounter only but in that moment my sense of self began to return.

I was sent into the library one evening at six with a tray, and found him there alone. Almost the whole company had been hunting that day and most of them were by then resting in their rooms. But Mr Ogilvy was lying back before the fire.

I stood by the door looking into the room. I thought of my first visit to it, when Mr Ogilvy had appeared as my saviour against the terrors of the marble statuary in the entrance hall; and since that time I had spent many hours there alone dreaming of the day when I would be grown up. But those dreams I no longer dreamt. I stood looking at the vast room, the great glowing fire, the shadows in the corners, the shelves lined with leatherbound volumes which seemed now to mock me—how could a creature like you allow yourself such thoughts?

Mr Ogilvy turned his head. "Come in, come in," he said and I jumped forward, almost tripping in my eagerness.

I put the tray down next to his elbow. All this time I had not looked him in the face, but had kept my eyes cast down in true housemaidly fashion, "respecting my betters". But then he said, "It's Harriet, isn't it?"

I bobbed a curtsey. "Yes, sir."

"Ah good," he said. "You see then, I remember."

His voice was warm. I could observe the warmth but it could not reach me in my worn down and broken state. "Remember, sir?" I said.

"Hm," he said. "This is a different Harriet, is it not?"

I made no answer.

He spoke now as if to himself. "Well, at least I didn't leave her to starve . . . "

And then the voice broke out of me before I could stop it. "I wish you had," I said. "I wish you had," and I burst into tears.

I expected at any moment a hefty box about the ears, a cuff about the shoulders, and crouched myself together against the blows which were sure to come. But they did not come. And at last I raised my tear-sodden eyes to stare with all the hatred I could feel at Mr Ogilvy.

But he was looking away from me into the fire. He said, "I see that someone has been ill-treating you. If it occurs again, you must speak of it to Mrs Minim."

"Yes, sir," I said. What use was that? I had simply been punished. Mrs Duckham would probably have sent me to the constables for what I had done. I made to escape from the room.

"Oh, and Harriet," he said, still not looking in my direction, still not raising his voice. "At present it is not possible, with so much company in the house; but when we are all away again, you may use the library as much as you like. I shall give Mrs Minim instructions to that effect."

At that I held still. I looked round the room and saw that now the books no longer mocked me but seemed to look at me with calm and benign expressions. I said, "May I, sir? May I really?"

"Of course," he said, with perfect indifference. "This is my household and you are a part of it. You may indeed, Harriet, use my library."

That evening I went to wait upon Nina Sanctuary as usual. But I had begun to come back into myself. I observed her now with a very different eye, not the eye of love, or of wonderment, but of contempt. She was with her mother as she so often was; and again I took account item by item of the gross vulgarity of the appearance of Lady Sanctuary, the coarseness of the hair, the bulbous width of the nose, the jowled flesh around the neck; and now I no longer marvelled at how little mother and daughter resembled each other. For I could see only too clearly how, before many years were out, Nina and her mother would look like sisters. If only Mr Ogilvy could be made to see it too, I thought; and found, suddenly, that I was once again searching in my mind for plans, for ideas. Mr Ogilvy must not escape me.

Chapter Nineteen

THE MARRIAGE was announced.

Mrs Minim came into her room, her skirts bubbling around her. I was on my knees, brushing the carpet and raising with the brush little whirls of dust and grit which settled on my tongue, my face, my hair; yet I scarcely noticed the discomfort for the confusion of feeling which was within me.

"So," said Mrs Minim. "He is to marry her."

I did not look up; the news had already reached the kitchens.

"Everything is settled. They will go to London and they will be married there."

My brush continued to sweep. No it isn't, no they won't, no they WON'T, said the brush.

"But before that there is to be a ball. In celebration. Harriet, we must get to work."

I got up from my knees. Still she had not looked at me, which was as well for I was not yet able to keep my horror, my anger from showing on my face. Without speaking, I stood at her desk as she drew pen and paper towards her.

"So little time," she said. "He has given us so little time. But we shall be ready. Everything will be ready."

She fell immediately to the composition of the most copious lists. Mr Ogilvy's table was always generous—for this ball it was to be positively royal. Like Mrs Duckham, Mrs Minim felt a most wholehearted loyalty towards Mr Ogilvy and now the prospect of rendering him a greater service than usual put her into an ecstasy of delight. "You, Harriet," she proclaimed, "must go to Swithindale this afternoon and give the order for the invitations. They must be dispatched as soon as possible."

Even as I walked along the corridors back to the kitchens, I felt the excitement and disorder that was running through the house. There was noise everywhere, of banging doors, running feet, raised voices. The ball, the wedding, the wedding, the ball, no one knew which was the more exciting. In the kitchen Mrs Duckham in the aftermath of a fit of hysterics was being soothed by a large glass of brandy. "Ah," she sighed. "We are to have a mistress at last. The Honourable Nina Sanctuary. Oh my, oh my."

That afternoon I mounted the ponycart and drove to Swithindale with Harry. "So," he observed. "Mr Ogilvy is to marry. We'll see some changes now, I'll be bound."

I said nothing. My hands were clasped tight in my lap, my heart lay within my breast like a small, hard pebble. Whether I was more frightened than angry I did not know. Harry glanced at me and then away. "Get up, there," he called to the pony.

Once at Swithindale and with my errand done, I walked down the street to the Rectory. The news from Thirleby Hall had travelled fast, and I was stopped half a dozen times by passers-by. "Is it true, is it true?"

"Yes, it's true," I said, my face sullen; and then at least I could feel, dull within me, the satisfaction of seeing their eager looks turn to frowns of puzzlement. There would be no joy for me in this marriage and therefore I wanted no joy for anyone.

When I arrived at the Rectory Mrs Ponsonby was in the kitchen making apple pies. I stood in the doorway, looking round; the scene was exactly as I remembered it, Mrs Ponsonby smiling at me, putting back strands of hair with floury fingers, the next to smallest child, who had been the smallest when I was last there, running to pull at my skirt. Only Patrick was absent.

"Harriet," said Mrs Ponsonby. "Why have you not been to see us? You're almost a stranger."

I sat down beside the table. "I've been busy," I said, "there's been work." Harriet the kitchen maid was talking, not Harriet who had learned to read and who knew by heart the Kings of England.

For a moment Mrs Ponsonby said nothing, but continued to

roll and turn her pastry. All the sounds in the kitchen were familiar, the thud of the rolling pin, the hissing of the fire, the sounds of the children contentedly playing. But for once they had no comfort for me, for I had moved into a dark and frightening world. Overcome with fear, I put my head in my hands and burst into tears. "Mrs Ponsonby, what will become of me?"

The children gathered round to stare. I picked up one of them, which one I scarcely knew, and held its small body close to mine trying to gain some consolation from it. But there was none to be had.

Mrs Ponsonby put her hand on my shoulder. "There now," she said.

I stopped crying at last and wiped my eyes and nose on a scrap of handkerchief as I had learned to do in that very kitchen. Mrs Ponsonby said, "Has something happened?"

"You haven't heard?"

"But what?"

"He is to marry her—he is to marry Nina Sanctuary."

"Oh that," she said. "But, Harriet, Mr Ogilvy's marriage will not affect *you*."

I looked away from her. Of course, she could not possibly understand what it all meant to me unless I told her of the dreams I had never dared to describe to anyone, the dreams Nina Sanctuary had seemed to know of without being told. Nor did she know of the punishment that had been inflicted on me—the punishment which would be the first of many if I stayed on at Thirleby Hall with Nina Sanctuary as its mistress. And if I did not stay there, where would I go?

"You know, Harriet," said Mrs Ponsonby. "You are coming to an age now where you may soon marry yourself."

"Me?" I said. "Me marry? But who will marry me—a foundling child?"

My voice rang out over the chatter of the children. Startled, they looked round and the baby on the instant began to cry. Without looking, I put out my hand to the cradle and began to rock it. The baby hiccuped and fell silent.

"But, Harriet," said Mrs Ponsonby. "It is the will of God. Through the goodness of Mr Ogilvy you have already had a far better life than you could have expected. Now you must live out your life in that station to which our good Lord has felt disposed to call you."

"But this is not my life," I said. "I am not a servant. It is not my nature to be a servant."

Mrs Ponsonby looked at me sadly. "My dear Harriet," she said. "Now I see that the wildness is still in you. And we worked so hard here, you and I, to drive it out."

"Is it wildness," I said, "to want to live?"

"Harriet," said Mrs Ponsonby, "now the devil in you is speaking. You must accept the will of our Lord and you must fight the devil within you which questions His will."

I looked up at the worn face, the tired hands. I thought how much I had always loved this face and yet now, I knew, I must reject it. For the sake of my survival.

Abruptly I stood up and Mrs Ponsonby, who had been leaning towards me, took a startled step backwards. For a moment I saw fear on her face and the sight delighted me. "So," I said. "It is the good Lord who would keep me humble, a creature, a servant. And it is the devil himself who tells me to be strong and the person I want to be. Then there is nothing I can do but renounce the Lord and all His works. I am the child of the devil and I must do as he bids."

A seed of certainty had been born. I was the devil's child, I knew it then, and as the devil's child I had great forces on my side. They were forces that did not always triumph and would, if I believed Mr Ponsonby's sermons, be vanquished for ever at the Last Trump; but the Last Trump seemed to me to be a very long way away and what I wanted was victory then, however shortlived. I still bore on my arm the scar made by the teeth of a rat, the mark of my old punishment; now it seemed to me this was the proof that the devil had that day entered into me. The continuing scar was the sign of his possession.

Chapter Twenty

A SENSE of calm, of happiness even, descended upon me in those days. For once I did not have to busy myself with any plans, for I had old Nick himself on my side. All the servants were working hard to prepare for the ball, rising earlier than usual, retiring later, and some of them began to grumble; but I neither complained, nor was aware of any fatigue; instead I worked with boundless energy and I even sang as I went about the house.

I caught some puzzled looks from my new mistress, Nina Sanctuary, in those days, and I thought that she was surprised at how much I seemed to have changed. No more resentful looks, only smiles; until she seemed to lose interest in me, as if I were a dog that had at first been noticed because it refused its training; but then, having been tamed, was no longer remarkable.

When the day of the ball arrived, she gave me to iron the dress she proposed to wear. It was a creation of white silk, the skirt decorated with numerous knots of blue ribbon, every one of which would have to be neatly pressed. "You're trusting it to *her*?" said Lady Sanctuary.

"Why not?" said Nina. She did not glance at me as she spoke, but nevertheless, as if she had, I curtseyed in her direction and gave a simpering smile. With every day that passed her fate came nearer and, ready and waiting as I was for that, I could afford to smile.

In the kitchen the servants gathered round to gape at the dress. "You wish it was yours, eh, my fine lady?" said Mrs Duckham. I shrugged and did not bother to reply as I went to get the irons ready. One day, and I was sure of it, even finer dresses than that would be mine.

When the irons were hot, I picked one up, weighing it carefully in my hand. How splendid it would be, I thought, to put an iron through the dress, to ruin it as I wanted to ruin her; but to do that would be to bring punishment upon myself and I wanted no more punishment.

That evening on the stroke of nine the orchestra, grouped in the front hall, struck up a rousing tune. From the gallery above I looked down on the flaring candles, the swirling skirts of the dancers. I could see Nina Sanctuary in the dress I had so carefully pressed; her shoulders and half her bosom were left bare by the silk and she was wearing a glittering necklace. I had never seen her look so fine and gazing down at her I felt for a moment a sense of misgiving. She was so strong; if I had the devil on my side, what powers might she not have on hers? But then the hatred swelled inside me, and I felt again the old certainty—she would not live, she could not live, I would not let her live. The flowers that had been banked round the walls filled the air with their sweet stench; for once the gardens of Thirleby Hall had not alone been able to meet the needs of the occasion and flowers had been sent from all the neighbouring estates, dahlias, chrysanthemums and a few exquisite, late-blooming roses. Such flowers would come too for her funeral.

Once the supper had been served, there were celebrations in the kitchens too, for the servants. A fiddler had been provided and there was enough beer for us all to drown in. The great house resounded with light and gaiety; in the front hall the gentry drank their wine, in the servants' quarters their coachmen sang and caroused with the rest of us. I drank and danced with abandon; Mrs Duckham had been drunk from the early afternoon, as much with beer as with exhaustion, and now she sat in her rocking chair beating time to the music and slapping her knees in jubilation. I went tearing past her on the arm of one of the grooms; "Hattie, my girl, you're dancing like a demon," she shouted, for once approving of me; and I waved and smiled to show that I had heard.

We got to bed, all of us, only as the cocks were crowing. Yet scarcely had I fallen asleep than I began dreaming of Steepleton Fair, of the horses, the gypsies. Whether I dreamt of what I had seen, or whether it was the tales I had heard that I remembered, I do not know. "Easy enough to make a slow one run frisky—or a frisky one run wild," said a voice in my ear, and I saw Nina Sanctuary mounting her favourite mare, with burrs under the saddle and under the tail enough to madden a dray horse. I heard the mare whinny in pain, I saw her rear; with anger on her face the rider tightened the reins, but still the animal danced until at last it took off at a terrifying speed out into the park.

And then the mist closed around both mount and rider; and I woke sweating with all I had drunk the night before in the gray, clear light of morning.

I had fallen asleep in my clothes, I discovered, and remembering the carousing of the night before, that did not surprise me. But the hem of my dress was wet and daubed with mud; and for that I could not guess the reason.

The dreams of the previous night had been so strong that they were still with me; I could hear the neighing of the horses, the rattle of impatient hooves. From my dreams—or had I somehow heard those noises through the early morning?

I had overslept; yet no one had come to waken me. As I walked down the back stairs the house was very quiet by contrast with the noise and revelry of the night before. And when I reached the kitchens I found that they were quiet too. There was only Dora, working at the dirty pots of the night before.

I had assumed much of Mrs Minim's authority by this time, at least as far as the younger maids were concerned.

"Are the breakfasts done?" I demanded.

Dora nodded her head. And then I saw that the creature's eyes were red with crying. "What's wrong now, Dora?" I asked impatiently.

"You don't know?" she said.

"No," I said. "What is it?" But even as I spoke the certainty began to grow.

"She's dead—the young lady is dead." And she burst into tears.

I felt a throbbing in my arm and, looking down, I saw that the scar was raised and livid. The devil had done his work.

Chapter Twenty-one

THE STORY was told a million times over; it is told to this day.

Very early that morning when the dancing was over they had gone out to ride. While I slept and dreamed of Steepleton Fair, Mr Ogilvy and his bride-to-be were galloping across the parkland, ridding themselves gloriously of the fumes and fatigues of the night before. It was a fine morning in October, bright except for small patches of mist. Nina, racing ahead of her lover, had been swallowed up in mist and the horse, as if in fear of something or someone, some strange shape appearing before it, had shied in fright and bolted. Nina Sanctuary had been hurled to the ground and instantly killed. But her hands were trapped in the reins and her body was dragged half a mile along the muddy earth before it was released.

When the mist cleared, the parkland where she had galloped was quite empty. There were no trees, no hedges, nothing to make a horse shy and bolt, except the mist itself.

She was buried at Thirleby Hall in the family vault beneath the chapel.

Chapter Twenty-two

NO ONE expected Mr Ogilvy to stay at Thirleby Hall after the death of his bride. "He'll be off back to Italy, I'll be bound," said Mrs Minim; and a tear found its way down her furrowed cheek.

But Mr Ogilvy did not return to Italy, nor did he speak of returning. He seemed to have lost his old delight in travelling and his life became quieter than I had ever known it. He went riding and hunting as he had done in the past, but he no longer went to London and he did not go abroad. He had never entertained a great deal at the house and now all the regular callers came on business concerned with the estate.

"He's changed, poor gentleman," said Mrs Duckham, and this was true. And as Mr Ogilvy changed, the house too seemed a different place, quiet, shrunken. Mr Ogilvy used the library almost exclusively and gave orders that the other state rooms were to be shut up. And so they were, the shutters closed, the furniture and the carpets put under dustcovers, so that the front of the house had a melancholy, unlived-in air, and the back of the house too was affected by the general atmosphere of mourning, the dark corners seeming more numerous and more obscure than ever. The young housemaids went up to bed only in clusters, and even Mrs Duckham preferred to be accompanied on the long journey to her bedroom under the eaves of the house.

Both the health and the spirits of Mrs Minim were

deteriorating rapidly. She spent most of her time in her room, often asleep. I had already assumed many of her duties; gradually I took on more and more of them, in her name at first, as if she were still capable of giving me the necessary orders, then taking her authority more and more openly.

All my care, my thought was for Mr Ogilvy. Under my direction Mrs Duckham prepared him the most delicate and tempting dishes and I insisted that Edward serve him every evening with some of the finest wine from the cellars. He had undergone a most dreadful shock; but I knew that with care, and in time, he would recover.

During these months, while I served him devotedly, he seemed to have no recollection of who I was; the child whom he had first brought to the house and even given a name had disappeared altogether from his mind. I was in his company every day, but he never called me by my name and often he scarcely seemed to see me. But I knew that I had only to wait.

In those days I went walking in the woods much less often than I had done in earlier years. Like the house, the trees seemed to have turned in upon themselves. Where once I had gone strolling, lifting my face to the sun and to the air, watching, with amusement, the busy preparation of the birds for spring, I now walked swiftly, feeling the menace of the bent branches, wondering what strange creatures might be concealed in the dark hollows of the trees.

One afternoon I came out onto the track above the woods. I felt glad to be away from the trees, feeling that some danger had threatened and been averted. I decided to take the long path back to the house, rather than returning through the trees, and I began walking as fast as I could.

From behind me I heard in the distance the sound of hooves as a horse came rapidly down the track. I glanced round, expecting to see Harry the groom returning from an errand, but at first the horse was too far distant for me to see who the rider was. I could tell only that his head was bent, his shoulders hunched, and that he wore a dark cloak which, filled with the wind, flew up behind him.

I walked on, feeling again fear beginning to grow in me for no reason that I knew. So, I found myself thinking, must travel the Angel of Death, swiftly, darkly, through the countryside; and I knew that one day the Angel of Death would appear to me and his face would look into mine. How would that face look, I wondered? Would it be gentle and benign, a welcoming face, or would it, in its dark lines, foretell the punishment that was to be mine for all my wickedness? I found myself trembling with terror at the thought, the wound on my arm beginning instantly to throb. Then I started to run jerkily, for I was already, for fear, out of breath; and the next moment I tripped over a dead log lying across the path and fell to the ground.

I could only lie there and hope that I might go unnoticed by the rider. But I heard the hooves slowing down. I crouched even lower, in fear, until I heard a voice and felt a hand on my shoulder. It was Mr Ogilvy.

"Are you ill? What the devil?" he demanded.

"It's nothing, sir, I tripped," I said. Leaning against the log, I got as rapidly as I could to my feet.

When he saw me standing he paused no longer but swung himself up on to his horse without a word. I watched him galloping away, knowing that he had had no idea at all who I was. And remembering the last time I had seen him in the woods, my heart filled with sadness. Then he had walked beside his love; then he had paused beneath the reaching branches of the trees to take her in his arms. Now in haste he rode away, leaving me to walk on alone.

That evening, after I had served him his good dinner and seen to the locking up of all the store cupboards, I took a candle and walked up the main staircase and along the corridor to the yellow and white bedroom.

To this room Mr Ogilvy had carried the broken body of his bride; here it had lain on the four poster bed until the day of the funeral. I myself had helped to dress her in death; she had worn a simple white garment and on the day of her funeral she had never looked more beautiful. In death, the greed, the covetousness of the curve of her mouth, the flare of her nose, had all disappeared; her face had had the innocence of a child and the terrible beauty of an angel.

Mr Ogilvy's orders had been that the room should not be shut up as so many other of the apartments had been, but left as it was, the bed ready for sleep, the draperies in place. I had followed his orders, but left the carrying out of them to the other maids; since that day I had not entered the room. Until now.

I opened the door and went in raising the candlestick high above my head. I had come here to this room, to the room where she had beaten me so savagely, to show her that I was not afraid and to show her, what was more, that I intended to take for myself what had been hers.

In every respect the room was ready for its mistress to take possession of it, even to the new candles in place on either side of the dressing-table. I dared to light these new candles, as if I myself were indeed the new mistress, and then I sat down before the glass, as I had never been able to do in her lifetime. I leant forward and tilted the mirror so that I could see my face clearly; and I studied my countenance.

I remembered everything about her. I had forgotten nothing, although it was now many months since her death. How clear the large blue eyes had been, how pale and unblemished the skin, although as Edward testified she drank as much as any gentleman. The hands had been small and white and most beautiful of all the hair, the long , silky chestnut hair. All this I conjured up before my eyes, quite calmly, item by item; and then I looked at my own face.

My hair, brush it though I did, was dull and coarse compared with hers. My skin was brown and already on my forehead there was a furrow. All these things I noticed; and yet, little dull brown thing that I was, I lifted my face proudly to the mirror, knowing that within me there was a power which would, there was no denying it, win me in the end everything that I desired.

And suddenly the door flew open, so fiercely that it banged against the opposite wall. Wind filled the room. Round the bed the draperies billowed and the curtains pressed against the glass. Still looking into the mirror I found my head pushed forward into my own image so that it was only by exerting all my strength that I prevented myself from smashing the glass into which I was looking. But I continued to hold my head an inch from the glass as wave after battering wave of wind hurled itself against the back of my head. I put out my hands to grip each side of the dressing-table and I shouted into the mirror, "Go—go back to the dead earth where you belong. Your time is finished." And as I spoke so the mirror was filled with colours, her colours, the chestnut of her hair, the whiteness of her skin, the blue of those celestial eyes. But I held on with all my strength, pitting the force of life against the power of the dead; and I heard at last behind me a small, sighing cry of surrender.

All was still. I picked up my candle and left the room.

Chapter Twenty-three

THE MONTHS passed. Spring came and the fresh clear sunlight entered the windows to light up the dusty corners of the house. By now I was housekeeper in all but name and it was I who decided that that year the house should receive an especially thorough spring cleaning. Every drapery in the house was taken down and washed, floors were re-waxed, the chandeliers were cleaned.

As much as I could, I left Mr Ogilvy undisturbed, and he seemed scarcely ready to disturb himself, so much a creature of habit had he become. I watched him and I waited for the right moment to present itself.

It was a late spring and not warm, but the chill winds brought with them smells of earth and freshly budding flowers. I came down out of the woods early one evening with bunches of wild daffodils and jonquils and I looked at the windows of the Hall glittering in the sunlight, and I felt as fresh and alive as the flowers I carried. The death of the year was over, it was time to forget even Nina Sanctuary. She had been beautiful and I was plain; but I was alive and I felt myself full of love.

I had made a habit of coming quietly into the library as if into a church. But on that evening I made up my mind to behave differently.

I had profited from the months of delay. My hair was brushed smooth into a rich dark brown. My hands no longer suffered from heavy work and the nails were polished. And my eyes, as I knew from every glass I passed, were large and eager, their depths telling of the depth of my feeling. On my body there was only one blemish: the scar on my arm which would never properly heal but this I kept covered and no one knew of it except myself.

I had placed a bowl on the library table containing some of the flowers I had gathered in the woods—the small, sweet wild daffodils, the pale narcissi. These were a sign of my intention. That evening when I brought his dinner, I spoke to him. "Your dinner, sir."

He did not turn from where he sat before the fire. I noticed that his hair was a good deal grayer than it had once been and that his shoulders were hunched. I went forward. "Sir," I said again.

I had moved quickly, abruptly, and the old dog at his feet must have been caught unawares, for he leapt up and towards me, snarling. His jaws were empty, for he had not a tooth in his head, but I was taken aback nevertheless. "Down," I said, only to find my hand seized between the drooling jaws; and I let out a cry of alarm.

Now Mr Ogilvy looked round and snapped out a word of command to the dog. I stood holding my bruised hand, less hurt than startled. "Brutus," said Mr Ogilvy to the dog. "This is no stranger—this is Harriet Dark."

So he did know me, he did remember. My pleasure at his remembering was enough to make me quite forget the pain in my hand. The dog continued to growl and regard me with suspicion, but I smiled joyfully at Mr Ogilvy.

I said, "Yes, sir, it's Harriet Dark."

"And now, Harriet, you are become a woman," he observed.

"Yes, sir," I said. And then, still smiling, "I brought you these flowers, sir, from the woods. Spring flowers."

I held out the bowl towards him. For a moment he looked at them and then up at me and almost began to smile. And then he leant forward and knocked the bowl out of my hand.

"This house shall see no spring," he said. "This is a house of mourning; and so it shall remain."

But I continued to stand calmly before him, knowing that I stood as straight as a young tree and with as much life in me. I said, "Yes, sir, I understand, sir," and could only hope that he would feel the contrast between the message I spoke and the meaning in my eyes.

The following morning I pulled back the curtains all over the house so as to let in the light and I put spring flowers all over the house. "It's the master's orders, is it?" asked Mrs Duckham, hearing the instructions I was giving to the maids.

"Of course," I retorted, hoping that any protest he might make would be for my ears alone. But in spite of what he had said the night before he made no protest, seeming to accept what I had done just as he had accepted the care I had given for the previous many months.

But it was a long time before he spoke to me again; until one evening in summer when I entered the library at his dinner hour to find him on his feet and looking towards the door as I entered.

He said, "You may remain here while I dine. I feel the need of company."

"Yes, sir," I said.

He motioned to me to sit down and then poured some wine looking critically at the glass, but there was only the polish to admire. Under my supervision the maids did their work well. He took a sip of the wine and then began drinking the soup, a good, clear broth, delicately flavoured with fresh herbs. "And what of Mrs Minim?" he said.

"She has not been well, sir, for some time."

"Indeed? I trust she is well looked after."

"Of course, sir."

He pushed aside his plate. "So my house is being run by a foundling child."

"I trust you find it well run, sir."

"I do, indeed." His face, which for many months had been grim and dark, took on now a softer look, a look of kindness. "So, Harriet," he said. "I did right to bring you here—after all."

Chapter Twenty-four

I KNEW that a turning point had been reached; but I also knew that I could not expect a straight path to my fulfilment and that there were likely to be many obstacles in the way.

And so it proved to be. There were evenings when he allowed me, and even wished me, to sit on in the library before the fire, after he had dined, while he talked to me of the countryside he knew so well and of his own life. But on other occasions he would wave me away and I knew that to stand my ground would do me no good at all.

How much I prized those evenings of our companionship. As Mrs Ponsonby years before had told me, Mr Ogilvy was a cultivated man indeed who could talk of so many things which I knew little of and that little from books alone. But Mr Ogilvy had begun to travel as a young man, doing a Grand Tour of Europe and had then conceived a love for the ancient cities and splendours of Europe which had increased as he grew older. For himself he had seen the temples of Greece, the ruins of Ancient Rome, and he was able to describe them to me in a way which made me long to see them too.

One evening in autumn we sat before the library fire while outside the rain spattered down. Mr Ogilvy had been talking of Rome, of how in the dog days of August, a dull and heavy heat lay over the city, feared as much by the Romans themselves as by foreign visitors. I found it difficult to imagine such heat; certainly I did not believe I had ever experienced such warmth, having spent all the life I could remember in the Yorkshire countryside and I sat, my needlework neglected in my lap, as I thought of how strange it must feel.

"No, indeed," said Mr Ogilvy decisively. "At all costs Rome is to be avoided then, in Ferragosto—" and then his gaze fell on me and he looked quite astonished at what he had said for, it was clear enough, for the time being he had forgotten who his companion was.

And realizing that it was time to leave him to himself, I got up and wished him a good night.

The time I spent in the library with Mr Ogilvy had not gone unnoticed in the kitchens by Mrs Duckham or by Edward the butler. Mrs Duckham was less ready, these days, to criticize me to my face, but many were the remarks meant for my hearing which were made just as I was leaving the kitchen or just as I was about to enter it. "Master and servant is like oil and water," she would sniff. "They don't mix and they was never meant to. A place for every one and every one in that place—that's the law of the Almighty."

I was aware myself that the heights of ambition which I daily approached in my fantasy were dazzlingly high and I could imagine what the servants would say if they knew of them. What laughter, what ridicule it would provoke if it were known for certain that I, Harriet Dark, saw myself as meeting on equal terms the master of Thirleby Hall. How could I set myself up next to a gentleman, and a very well-to-do gentleman, who had been pledged to marry one of the most beautiful young ladies in England.

And yet I knew that there was another truth, not acknowledged by the world, in which I was the equal of Mr Ogilvy, and that was in strength. Like him I was strong and I was passionate. My physical strength might be less but I knew myself to be his equal in determination and even in intellect. And I meant to prove that I was.

In those days Mr Ogilvy was left almost completely to me for his old friends seldom came to the house. At first they had kept away out of respect, then as he lingered in his grief, they became impatient, until now he seemed forgotten by the world, except for his own household. He had only one regular caller and that was the Reverend Ponsonby.

When the Reverend Ponsonby was in the house I kept myself in the background; for some reason that I did not clarify even to myself, I did not want him to know of the friendship which had developed between myself and Mr Ogilvy; perhaps I knew that like Mrs Duckham and for not dissimilar reasons he would disapprove of it and perhaps, however I explained my ambitions, I was not as contented by them myself as I pretended to be. For whatever reason, when the Reverend Ponsonby was present, I remained in the housekeeper's room or in the nether regions of the house.

But one day, when I knew that he had called, I was summoned by one of the maids to the library; I made sure my dress and my hair were in place—I was wearing that day a smooth dress of black silk which had been made up for me in Swithindale with a fine trimming of white lace around the neck, and I knew that I was looking very well indeed. What did Mr Ogilvy want with me, I wondered?

He and Mr Ponsonby were not alone. As I entered the room, I saw a little group of people standing at the far end of the room around the fireplace. There was, as I expected, the Reverend Ponsonby redfaced as always, and beside him my dear Mr Ogilvy looking, as he did in those days, a good deal more upright and cheerful. The worst days of his mourning were certainly over. But next to Mr Ogilvy were two people whom I did not recognize.

I saw first a young man who, as I entered, turned towards me. Until then it had been a rough, stormy day; the sky had been filled with cloud and the house had seemed gloomier than usual. But as the young man looked towards me, a shaft of sunlight pierced the cloud and came through the high window to rest against his pale hair and countenance. So, for a moment, I could not distinguish his features; I could see only a halo of light, and startled I stopped quite still. If Mr Ogilvy, coming through the woods had seemed an Angel of Death, then certainly I was being visited now by an Angel of Light.

I stood staring and bemused; until someone, a young girl, came forward out of the group and took my hand. It was Maria Ponsonby. "Harriet," she said laughing. "Have we changed so much? Do you really not know us?"

And then the young man came forward too to shake me by the hand and at last I realized that of course I knew him. It was Patrick, Patrick Ponsonby, returned from school, from university and now grown up.

Before I knew what I was saying, I blurted out, "I can read now." Patrick laughed and once again the sunlight catching the fair skin, fair hair, turned him all to gold. "But, my dear Harriet, you are a most accomplished young lady, I feel sure."

Like his father Patrick was to be ordained and, as I discovered later from Mr Ogilvy, his father had brought him to Thirleby Hall to discuss with Mr Ogilvy whether a suitable living might be found for him. I had been summoned to the library at Maria's request. "Dear Harriet, we never see you now," she said, pressing her hand against mine.

"My household duties," I began; and Mr Ogilvy said, "What would I do without Harriet? She is the best housekeeper this house has ever had."

I was grateful that he had prevented me from going on. For my duties had rarely in fact stopped me from doing anything that I wanted to do. But ever since the death of Nina Sanctuary and the passionate declaration I had made to Mrs Ponsonby before that event of my being the devil's child, I had felt it as well to keep away from the Rectory. For I had spoken the truth to Mrs Ponsonby, as I knew it, and I felt sure that when those kindly, discerning eyes met mine again, she would know that it had indeed been the truth. And would she see also what had been the truth of Nina's death? That I found a thought too terrible to contemplate.

While Mr Ogilvy and Mr Ponsonby talked over glasses of fine sherry and biscuits newly baked by Mrs Duckham, Patrick, Maria and I strolled before the house. The grass was smelling from the rain and now that the sun had come out, the day was turning warm. How much I rejoiced in the presence of my old friends. Patrick had been far, so very far, since those days of our lessons in the Rectory kitchen—to school and then to Oxford. He had even been abroad to France and to Italy, as companion to a young lord on a Grand Tour. I felt envy awakening in me.

"And all this while I have been here," I sighed, turning to look up at the broad and generous face of Thirleby Hall.

What had kept me here? Certainly I had had no chance of going elsewhere, but more than that my devotion to Mr Ogilvy had been the dominant force holding me in my place, depriving me even of the wish to go away. But Patrick had been free and able to travel. I found myself sighing, just a little, and puckering my lip in discontent.

Beside me Maria laughed. "Dear Harriet, you have not changed," she said. "Even all those years ago you always wanted to do everything that Patrick did. Do you remember?"

"Did I?" I said, marvelling. I looked at Patrick and he looked back at me, smiling. "And you did," he said, "when it was a question of reading and writing."

Of course—reading and writing. Strange to think that once simply to read and write had been my goal, that I had seen these simple abilities as my passport to unimaginable riches. I could indeed read and write and since then I had acquired other skills too. And yet here I was still at Thirleby Hall, while Patrick had become educated and had travelled over half Europe. "You really went to Florence," I said, "and to Rome?"

"Indeed I did," he said. "And I was tempted to turn Catholic. Harriet, you cannot conceive of the beauty of the churches, the dignity of the worship—"

But Maria, looking half-frightened, interrupted him. "Patrick," she said, shushing him, finger to her lips. "You must not say such things, or even think them."

Patrick smiled. "Maria, our church is changing—and for the better. You know nothing up here in Swithindale, but in the south my opinions are commonly shared even by dignitaries of the church."

"But it would so upset Father to hear such talk—"

"Father," said Patrick, "must learn that I am no hunting parson, though I am his son."

I looked from one to the other, feeling once more the envy that I had felt as a child of the closeness of brother and sister. I had had no one, not even a mother, when I was a child; now, as a young woman I still had no one—except for Mr Ogilvy.

Maria turned back to me. "Harriet," she said, "I had to see you this morning—to say goodbye. Now that the little ones are older and Patrick is back, at least for a time, I am leaving Swithindale."

"You too?" I said. It seemed that everyone left, sooner or later; and I was the only one who always remained behind.

"Yes," she said. "I am to go to Halifax, to become a governess."

I saw that her mouth was trembling, even while she looked at me with firm and resolute eyes. I said, "Shall you like that?"

"I have no choice," she replied. "Now that I am no longer needed at home, it is my duty to earn a living."

Patrick was frowning down at the gravel path. "It will not be for long, Maria," he said. "As soon as I am settled, you shall come and live with me. I shall need someone."

"Ah," said Maria. "But by then you may have a wife."

There was a pause. Of course, I thought, Patrick might

indeed marry, and soon. I wondered who would be his choice, and I felt that I knew the answer. It would be someone gay and young like himself, someone sweet and demure like Maria and certainly it would be a lady. I put my hand to my arm, where beneath the cloth of my sleeve I could feel the raised scar of my old wound.

We turned back to the house and found that Mr Ogilvy and the Reverend Ponsonby were standing on the steps looking towards us. It was evident that the morning's business had been concluded and that Mr Ponsonby was ready to depart. In the house a dozen small tasks waited for me as they did every day of the week; but friends coming to visit me had made this a most extraordinary day. I could scarcely bear to think that when they had left I would return to my store cupboards and my inventories as usual.

Maria kissed me. "Please visit Mother at Swithindale," she said. "She speaks of you often and with such fondness."

At her soft touch, her loving words, I felt my face growing instantly dark. What had I to do with fondness, with affection? I was the devil's child, self-declared, self-appointed perhaps, but most certainly the devil had been present at my inauguration and had confirmed me in wickedness.

Patrick and Mr Ogilvy were shaking hands. I looked at the two men, standing side by side; Patrick was all light, all golden clarity, while Mr Ogilvy, my Mr Ogilvy, was dark, thickset and saturnine, as mysterious in visage as I knew my own secrets to be.

Chapter Twenty-five

IT WAS becoming clear to everyone that Mr Ogilvy's condition had very much improved—that he was almost his own self again. "It's good to see the master looking gradely," said Mrs Duckham. "No doubt he'll be off on his travels again before long."

Her eyes, those coarse, red-rimmed eyes, slid round towards me as she spoke; my own eyes looked steadfastly down at the day's menus in my hands but nevertheless I could feel her gaze greedy against my cheeks. Betsey said, "You think so, do you, Mrs Duckham?"

"Oh I do. After all, there's nothing to keep him here, is there?"

She turned back to the kitchen range to sample one of the enormous pots of soup bubbling there. Once I would have aimed a good kick at her and now the impulse to plant my foot judiciously amongst her voluminous skirts was still there; but by this time I had learned more subtle ways of knocking her from her perch, ways which would not rebound to my own discredit. I said sweetly, "I have a new receipt here, Mrs Duckham, for caramel custard. I should be glad if you would try it for the master."

Her already flushed face turned a dull red with annoyance. She was an excellent cook but all her skill was in her hands; she had never learnt to follow a recipe—for that matter she could barely read. It would take her all afternoon to make a caramel custard according to written instructions and it might well turn out a good deal less palatable than the dish she made herself with a dash of spirits, a sprinkling of vanilla. But she would never admit as much to me, the jumped-up kitchen maid, and instead she now took the piece of paper I handed to her and did her best to look at it as if all its symbols made instant sense.

"Thank you, Mrs Duckham," I said and departed for the housekeeper's room.

This room was now entirely mine, for Mrs Minim had retreated to her bed. It was plain she had not much time to live; she spent most of her days asleep and when she was awake her mind was confused. She seemed to be quite certain that Mr Ogilvy had married Nina Sanctuary; she spoke of the beautiful young mistress who now reigned at Thirleby Hall. "Serve her well, Harriet," she would say.

It was useless to try to explain to her that she was talking nonsense; indeed by this time very little of her seemed to be remaining in this world, almost all having gone on to the next. I kept her as comfortable as I knew how, feeding her on Mrs Duckham's good strong beef tea, and the doctor from Swithindale visited her from time to time, but it was clear that little could be done for her and she seemed very little aware of our efforts to make her last days of life pleasant ones. She lay, stragglehaired and wasted against the pillows, almost unrecognizable when compared with the imposing, authoritative figure I remembered from my early childhood.

And seeing her loss of strength, knowing how near death was to her, I felt a terrible foreboding, less for her than for myself. She was too clear a reminder to me of what one day I would become when my youth and strength, the youth and strength I now so gloried in, would be gone. How would I face my Maker—I who had made a covenant with the devil? But I could not go back on that covenant, for so far what I most wanted from life I still had not received.

Mr Ogilvy and I were friends, companions by now, but gaining his companionship was only a stepping stone on the way to my goal. Eagerly, greedily, I sought always for more; I wanted there to be no corner of his being which I had not explored.

I did everything I could think of; as much as I could I kept myself there in the background of his life, efficient, unobtrusive. His valet now took orders from me, and I had even begun to acquire a fair knowledge of the workings of the estate. "Harriet," Mr Ogilvy would call ten times a day, and I was instantly at his side. "Heavens above," he would say, looking affectionately down at me, "how did I ever manage without you?"

It was part of my aim that he should not be able to manage without me; in this I seemed to be succeeding splendidly, increasing his dependence upon me. But this victory, great though it was, demanding skill on my part, was by no means enough to satisfy me. Mr Ogilvy, after all, was a gentleman and one of the things I had learned about gentlemen was their predisposition, even predilection for depending on those around them. Presumably they felt certain that there would always be people to serve them; and it was only those like myself who had grown up with nothing who could bear to rely on no one.

And of course I had seen Mr Ogilvy in love, plainly, blatantly in love. I had seen him crossing the hall to meet Nina, I had seen him take Nina in his arms, and so far I could not for a moment, even for a moment, believe that what Mr Ogilvy had felt for Nina he now felt for me.

But I did not give up hope. By now I realized that I had established myself as a constant companion and a most efficient servant; what I felt sure I needed to do was to make him see me not as a servant but as a woman who could stand beside him, who was worthy to stand beside him. He had to see that I had many other accomplishments besides those of the perfect housekeeper.

He spoke one evening of Hangerbury Hill, a place of reputed beauty some miles from Thirleby Hall.

"Hangerbury Hill?" I said. "I have never been there."

"But you should go, Harriet. It is a fine sight at this time of year, especially when the gorse is in bloom. On a clear day you can see as far as the coast."

"Have I your permission to borrow a horse, sir?" I asked.

He looked at me in surprise, as I had guessed he would. "A horse? You mean you can ride?"

"Yes, indeed, sir," I replied.

"Really," he said with a smile. "I see there is no end to the skills you have acquired in my house."

"I can ride, sir," I said again.

"Well," he said, "in that case you may ride there with me. Give instructions to Harry."

"Yes, sir," I said. "Thank you, sir."

But first I had to make a hasty visit to Swithindale. Maria

Ponsonby had ridden from a child and we were much of a size. She would surely have left a habit behind her at the Rectory which I could wear. For I had to have a respectable habit; I knew I could not hope to look as spectacular as Nina Sanctuary had done on horseback, but I could not ride at all beside Mr Ogilvy if I were not properly dressed.

The need to find a costume made me forget, for a moment, how much I disliked the thought of confronting Mrs Ponsonby again. I drove hastily into Swithindale in the trap and found myself before the Rectory door with no thought except that of finding myself a suitable habit.

The door was opened by Patrick. In my haste I had forgotten not only Mrs Ponsonby but also Patrick. In that moment I could only wonder how on earth it could have happened that I had forgotten Patrick.

He stood holding the door open. He looked very young, very strong and extraordinarily handsome; his smile was sweet indeed. "Harriet," he said and stretched out a hand to me.

In that moment I felt as if my heart was a lump of rock which had been touched by a ray of sunlight even in the midst of a winter's day. It was a new and altogether delightful sensation and for a moment I savoured it, marvelling at it as I did so. And then from behind came the voice of Mrs Ponsonby, that calm, benign voice. "Come along, children, good children," and I felt tears in my eyes. I was no good child and in this house of goodness there was no place for me.

I ignored Patrick's hand and stepped past him. "Mrs Ponsonby," I called. "I have come to ask you a favour."

Maria had indeed left a riding costume behind her and, "I am sure you may borrow it," said Mrs Ponsonby, "if it will fit. But what does this mean, Harriet, that you are to ride with Mr Ogilvy?"

I answered her sullenly without raising my eyes. "Mr Ogilvy is in need of company," I replied.

"Indeed, poor gentleman," she said with a sigh. "He has been mourning her for a long time."

"Not for much longer," I said. "Or so I believe," I added quickly, seeing the puzzlement on her face.

She left me to try on the habit. It scarcely fitted, but I pulled and pinned, resolving with my skilful needle to make it a good fit on my return to Thirleby Hall. I thought I did not make a bad sight and I went downstairs to show myself off.

"Harriet," said Mrs Ponsonby. "Now you look a lady."

Patrick stood behind her, observing me with a judiciously puckered lip. "Indeed you do, Harriet, but then I believe you have it in you to be something better than a lady. What is a lady after all but one who cannot earn her bread? You have within you a desire after truth and there is nothing more important."

Silence fell. I found myself looking at the floor, trying to hold back my tears. How little he knew about me, how very little.

Mrs Ponsonby was looking not at me but at her son. "Quite right, Patrick," she said. "You are proving to be a fine son."

Chapter Twenty-six

I REMEMBERED clearly seeing Nina Sanctuary set off with Mr Ogilvy for a morning's ride; while the horses pranced on the gravel path before the house, Mr Ogilvy would wait, splendid in his riding clothes and soft leather boots, his impatience obvious to all the world; and she would keep him waiting for as much as an hour before she came down the great staircase, smiling, her head held high. His irritation at once forgotten, he would go to her side and take her hand; and it was always she who would say at last, in that sweet, carrying voice, "Come then, Robert, the morning is already half spent."

And I, with the rest of the maids, would watch while the whole great cavalcade went off across the park; and then sighing turn back to our tasks.

My own departure with Mr Ogilvy took place from the stables and not from the front hall and I knew I could not rival Nina Sanctuary either in looks or in horsemanship. And yet the moment was full of satisfaction, nevertheless. I was to ride side by side with Mr Ogilvy, modestly mounted it was true, but riding beside him just the same; and there, at the kitchen door to watch us leave were Betsey and Dora , my old companions.

Behind them in the kitchen Mrs Duckham was snorting as she kneaded the bread, refusing to join in the excitement and Betsey did not know whether to applaud or to sneer; so in the end she did both and my last sight of her as we rode out of the yard was as she seized one of the stable brooms and waved it on high in an irreverent salute.

I can scarcely describe the happiness of that day, the joy of moving along on horseback next to Mr Ogilvy, seeing that dark face, marked with pain, gradually becoming lighter in its expression as the day went on. It was October, but the air on our faces was warm without the slightest touch of frost; and the touch of the sun was altogether benign.

We rode across country and I realized for the first time how great were the dimensions of the estate. Passing beyond the land farmed by Mr Ogilvy himself, we went cantering across the fields of the tenant farmers. Here and there we came very close to the farmhouses and the farmers' wives came to their doors to curtsey to Mr Ogilvy and the party from the hall; and around them, their ragged children stood gazing in wonderment, fingers in their mouths.

It was a ride of more than an hour, an invigorating ride, to Hangerbury Hill. We approached it across a broad, high plateau and then found ourselves at the rim of the hill, looking out across miles of descending country. Acres of yellow gorse stretched out before us, broken by trees in their autumn colours, bound by the distant blue ribbon of the sea. I felt that it was all mine, that because I stood there beside Mr Ogilvy the whole kingdom of the world was mine.

I had brought with us a basket of refreshments, cold chicken, fruit and wine. I knew how a lady would have enjoyed such refreshments spread out daintily upon a white cloth; but I rejoiced rather in partaking of them heartily, standing up, walking about like a gentleman beside Mr Ogilvy. I might never have tasted food before. "This chicken is—delicious," I found myself saying, thinking in the same moment what an impossibly inadequate word "delicious" was and how inadequate all words were to describe the taste, the texture of the food and the wine enjoyed on Hangerbury Hill on a brilliant day in October, beside Mr Ogilvy.

Riding home we came to a clear stretch of open ground. Without a word Mr Ogilvy put his horse to the gallop; I hesitated at first, for this morning's ride was the first practice I had had on a horse for many months; and then I too dug my heels into my horse's side.

The grooms continued to trot behind us and we were soon a distance ahead of them. What a life this was, I found myself thinking, the sun on my face, the open countryside around me.

How could I ever again accept a life enclosed by the back cupboards of Thirleby Hall? I kept my eyes on the dark rider in front of me; with him I felt sure lay my future and my life.

Coming up to a wood he slowed down and we both came to a halt. "Shall we skirt the wood, or shall we walk through it?" he asked me.

"A walk would be delightful, sir," I replied.

He dismounted and came over to help me down, smiling at my reddened face, looseflying hair. "You kept up well, Harriet," he said.

We walked into the wood between the trees, our footsteps loud against the quiet noises made by the woodland creatures. Birds flew above us, chattering; there were scurrying sounds of pattering feet.

He stopped suddenly and turned as if to speak. For a moment there was silence, which made me realize how alone we were. I raised my eyes to his face, willing him as passionately as I knew how to reach down and take me into his arms and, as our eyes met, it seemed as if that was what he would do. But then even as I lifted my face, I saw the figure of Nina Sanctuary; I saw him embracing her just as I had seen him do that day in the woods above Thirleby Hall. My lips grew stiff and cold and I drew back. He said, "Where are the grooms? They do not seem to be behind."

That evening, after our return, I went up to my room, took off the borrowed habit and lay down for a moment on the bed to rest and to think.

One thing was clear—that Nina Sanctuary be dead was not enough. Something more was needed, more of the devil's work, so that she would be not merely dead but blotted out of the past completely. Mr Ogilvy was still not free of her for the love he had borne her while she lived; and I was not free of her for the hatred which had found expression in her dying. Had he seen her between us in the woods, as I had done? Perhaps not, for he had made no sign. But I had known that she was there, between us.

What was I to do? For the moment I could not see, I could not tell. I felt the wound on my arm, stiff and raised, but it gave me no solution.

I got up at last and dressed in my neat black costume, fastening my collar with a small brooch of seed pearls which Mrs Minim had given to me years before. Once more I was become housekeeper—only my cheeks, glowing from the day's exercize, told that I was no houseborn creature, but one tamed to it by circumstance.

I prepared myself to return to my normal routine; I had tasted freedom that day and it had set off in me a gigantic appetite for liberty. But I could not for the moment imagine any possibility of that appetite being satisfied.

Chapter Twenty-seven

BUT IT was to be some days before my life did return once more to its familiar routine; before that time there occurred several events in my life of the greatest moment.

In the kitchen that evening everything appeared to be in order, as far as I could see; a vast piece of bacon was boiling for the servants' dinner and a good pair of chickens were roasting for Mr Ogilvy, as well as a trout. Mrs Duckham was sullen, responding to my queries with a grunt or a nod, but not daring, in the circumstances as she saw them, to show her resentment openly.

"Very good, Mrs Duckham," I said, and prepared to go to my room where, these days, I dined alone.

Then I heard a clamour from outside. "What is that noise?" I asked. Mrs Duckham muttered something I scarcely heard about jumped-up folks who would poke their noses in. Ignoring her, I went to the door.

There was a beggar woman in the yard. She was being driven away by pails of water while the farm mongrels snapped at her heels. As I reached the doorway, the woman turned her head to swear defiance at her tormentors; and her eyes for a moment flashed over me.

Even now I am not sure what happened in that moment. All I know is that the years fell away like so many leaves caught in a gust of wind. I was a child again, a very little child; all because of the pale blue eyes which shone out of a dirty, weatherbeaten old face.

Almost fainting I took a step back; and she began making off again as fast as her aged limbs would let her. "And good riddance," shouted one of the grooms, casually sending a stone through the air after her. It caught her on the back but no doubt for fear of worse that might come she did not stop.

I found my voice at last. "Are you all mad? She's not a dog to be driven away."

They turned to stare at me, laughter and surprise mingling on their faces. To them a dog was what she was and not a good farm animal but a stray who might steal or molest the livestock. And who was I to tell them different? It was I who was mad, not they.

But I knew I had Mr Ogilvy on my side. Mr Ogilvy maintained always a generous household before all comers. He would want no one driven from his door. Had he not taken me in as a child with nothing?

I crossed the stableyard towards the woman. She was a filthier hag than I had realized, seams of dirt running deep all along the lines of her face. The smell from her body and her clothes was putrid. She shrank back from me as if fearing that I too would strike her. I said, "Don't be afraid, tell me what you want here at Thirleby Hall."

A kind of smirk came now over her face. She said, in a highpitched, whining voice, "Nothing but a crust, mum. A house like this you must have a crust to spare."

I said, "Come into the house."

Mrs Duckham in the kitchen put her hands on her hips and opened her mouth to let loose a tirade of indignation. I cut her short. "A bowl of soup, please, Mrs Duckham and some bread. She can eat it here in the corner."

"Well, I—" began Mrs Duckham.

"Quickly," I said.

It was more than I could do to watch the creature eat. She slavered into the bowl, sticking chunks of bread into her mouth and then gulping into the soup so that at last the bread, softened, could be swallowed. Her teeth, black, were evidently no use for biting. Pretending to ignore her, I busied myself about the kitchen.

But I knew now why the sight of her had startled me so much. Her eyes, those extraordinarily flower-like eyes, gleaming in her face—those eyes were the eyes of my mother.

It was possible, I knew it was possible. This creature might indeed be my mother. I, Harriet Dark, for I knew no other name for myself, might be the daughter of this evil smelling woman who would have been driven away like a wild dog if I had not been there to prevent it.

I had always imagined that my mother must have died years before. But perhaps she had not died, perhaps she had gone on travelling, begging, to become the dreadful old hag who sat before me now grunting and sniffing into a basin of charitable soup.

She finished at last and then sat for a moment looking round the kitchen. She seemed to be smiling, but it was hard to tell; at any rate her mouth was open, the tongue lolling out. Mrs Duckham made a gesture of the hand towards her. "She'll be on her way now, I take it."

I said, "If you wish, old woman, you may spend the night in the stables here."

Mrs Duckham drew in her breath in horror. "Mr Ogilvy—"

"I will be responsible, Mrs Duckham," I replied.

I took the old woman out and put her with a good pile of sacking into one of the empty loose boxes. It was not what I would have wanted myself but it was a good deal better, I felt sure, than the bed she would have found out on the hills.

I could settle to nothing that night. Whatever I tried to do, the face of the old woman came before my eyes. Was she in fact my mother? Could I find out if she was really my mother? It was clear that she had not recognized me, but then my mother had last seen me as a small child.

For the first time I excused myself early in the evening from Mr Ogilvy's company, pleading an aching back.

"You should take more exercize, Harriet," he said. I thought I saw a faint look of disappointment in his eyes; even as this thought warmed me, I wondered what he would think if he knew... But that thought I shut out.

I waited in my room until the house was quite dark, quite silent. Then I took a candle and went down the stairs. I was not afraid of the darkness, for I knew that what secrets there were in the house were all mine.

The kitchen, clean and ready for the morning, was empty as I knew it would be. Gently I pushed back the bolts, opened the door and went into the yard.

The old woman, the sacking wrapped round her, was fast asleep. I stood looking down at her for a moment; all I could see was the pile of sacks, with some bedraggled strands of grey-white hair peeping out at the top. What could I say? Somewhere within me a child cried for its mother, a racking, harsh cry which I knew would never be stilled; I put out my foot and jabbed the old woman awake.

She awoke with a jerk. "What is it, what is it?"

I said, "Who are you? Why have you come here?"

"Nothing to you, just an old tinker woman." She looked bewildered now and anxious.

I said, "Have you ever had a child?"

"A child?"

"A girl—a girl that you left at Steepleton Fair."

"Not me, that wasn't me, I've never been to Steepleton Fair."

I said, "I want to know the truth—tell me."

It was plain my words meant nothing to her. She looked merely dazed, puzzled. How could I have expected otherwise? She was an old woman, half crazy.

But I had thought of another way. In my pocket I had a small piece of red ribbon, the only thing remaining to me from my mother. I held up the candle and thrust the ribbon into its light.

"Do you remember this, old woman, do you remember this?"

She looked up into the light still, for a moment, puzzled. I could scarcely bear the waiting as slowly, so slowly, she understood what she was being asked to look at. The puzzlement on her face continued for a while; but then there came a kind of recognition.

"Steepleton Fair," she said at last. "I remember—Steepleton Fair."

I ran as fast as I could. Down the yard and into the kitchen, pausing only to fling the bolts across the door. Sobbing, panting, I crashed up the backstairs to my room, not caring how much noise I spread through the silent house. Until I reached my bed.

My comprehension had ceased. I could understand nothing. For years I had cried myself to sleep, longing for my mother's warm body, my mother's soft touch. And now my mother had been found. And she was a hag from whom I could only draw back in horror and disgust.

My prayers had indeed been answered. By the devil himself.

Chapter Twenty-eight

I KNOW that I must have slept at last, for I found myself waking with a start, a sour, yellow taste in my mouth. I got dressed looking into the mirror as little as was necessary, for fear of what I might see there.

I was late going downstairs; the kitchen range was lit, the maids were about their work and so was Mrs Duckham. I walked past them all with only a brief good morning, and went out into the stableyard. I wanted to know my name, and that was all I wanted from her. That, surely, she would be able to remember.

But the box was empty. Only there still hung on the air the putrid smell of a body rotting even before death. I looked along the yard and up to the hills; but there was no sign of her.

"She's gone then," I said to Mrs Duckham.

"She's gone. And I don't reckon as she'll be back."

Her words barely reached the surface of my mind and I could not take in their meaning. Something perhaps had happened to the old woman while I lay in bed; or something perhaps had not. I did not feel that it concerned me.

The day went by on leaden feet. The malaise that had come to me in the early morning did not improve, instead it grew worse. I could taste no food and as for work I could settle to nothing.

Mr Ogilvy noticed my changed looks with concern. "Your back is still troubling you?" he suggested.

"Yes, sir," I replied, glad of the excuse.

How could I explain to him what had happened? He, of all people, must know nothing.

I sat, in the afternoon, before my accounts. The account book was generally a matter of great pride to me; in recent months Mr Ogilvy had looked at it only once and had smiled and said, "Excellent, Harriet, I see I can safely leave all this to you." So the accounts were to be scrutinized by no one but me and yet I took pleasure in making them immaculate, first working out the sums in rough and then transferring the checked totals to the fair white page. It was a soothing occupation, entering, checking; but that afternoon the figures ceased to make sense, and I found myself staring down at them the pen still in my hand.

There was a tap at the door.

"Yes?" I said.

"A visitor for you, m'm," said Dora.

"Oh?"

Patrick, smiling, windblown, was coming in through the door.

"Good afternoon, Harriet."

I stared at him. It was my mother I had expected to see coming in through the door, the ancient toothless hag who was my mother. And so for a moment I could not comprehend who had come instead.

"I may come in?" said Patrick gently.

"Of course, for a moment I thought—" Behind him Dora was hovering. I shut the door firmly after her.

"So, Harriet," said Patrick. "You have us all agog at the Rectory. How was your ride?"

He was standing leaning against the table. From a long distance away, it seemed, I felt his eyes on my face, their blue gaze as warming as on the previous day the October sunlight had been. And yet now that I had found my mother and knew myself all the better because of that, now the day before had become a very distant one.

I said, "It was very pleasant, thank you, Patrick."

"Ah," he said. "Good. I am glad to hear it. What a benevolent man Mr Ogilvy must be, to treat his housekeeper thus. At least, I assume that this is how he usually treats his housekeepers?"

"Mr Ogilvy and I are—"

"Yes?" he said.

I blushed. "Almost friends," I said at last.

"But you are still his housekeeper."

To that there was nothing I could say. Patrick turned away to examine the room, the plainly furnished room patterned with an old, dark-brown paper. There was almost nothing in the room which was mine; I had few possessions except for my clothes and so I had left on the walls miniatures belonging to Mrs Minim, and her most prized possession, a grandfather clock, stood in one corner. I became in that moment aware of the heaviness of its ticking. By then I had occupied the room for a year; how many more years would I spend there, I wondered?

I said, "Have you heard from Maria?"

"Indeed we have," said Patrick. "She appears to have settled down well—only that she is homesick from time to time. But she will visit us at Christmas and shortly papa is to visit her at Halifax."

I nodded. "I see."

And then, all of a sudden, I found Patrick leaning against my desk, his face very close to mine. "Harriet," he said, "you must tell me the truth. What is your feeling for Mr Ogilvy?"

I stammered. "I—I," I said. Then recovering my wits, "But what has that to do with you?"

"Harriet," he said again, smiling; and something of the meaning in that smile penetrated my wits, dull though they were. And once again there was a tap at the door.

"The master says, will you go into him, he's in the library," said Dora.

Patrick stood back. "Yes," he said. "My father is with him. We rode over together."

I patted my hair, smoothed down my skirt. "At once, Dora," I said. What had Patrick been about to say? Now it did not seem of the least importance.

"Ah, Harriet," said Mr Ogilvy. "And Patrick. I have just been talking to my good friend here. He has been reminding me of what a glorious time of year this is in Italy. And only today I received a letter from the factor concerning various problems which must be solved. I think I must go to Ravello."

Mr Ponsonby was rubbing his hands in satisfaction.

"Excellent," he said. "I see you are quite recovered."

Mr Ogilvy turned away for a moment. "Not altogether," he said, as if to himself. "There are some blows from which one can never quite recover. But . . . " and he turned back with a smile, "I am most certainly better and for that it is Harriet here who deserves the thanks."

I blushed for pleasure, looking at him with all the warmth I felt for him upon my face. He, as if feeling that some gesture was called for, stretched out his hand and gave me a kind of cuff on the arm. And with that gesture I saw him once more in the woods, leaning forward to embrace Nina Sanctuary. How differently.

"I recall, sir," said Patrick, "passing very close to Ravello. A fine spot indeed."

Around me the chatter rose and fell. I must have appeared composed, for no one remarked otherwise. But I felt as if my life as I had so far known it was coming to an end. The devil had given me my chance and I had not been able to take it; Mr Ogilvy, broken by Nina's death, had been mine all these months; I had restored him to life only to have to let him go.

"And when do you plan to travel, sir?" asked Patrick.

"Well," he replied, "everything is in excellent order here. I may well be able to leave within a day or two."

A cry of dismay rose to my lips. But only Patrick seemed to hear it, for only Patrick turned in my direction.

Mr Ogilvy was looking towards the Reverend Ponsonby. "About that living, Ponsonby, for your son. I believe that very shortly there should be good news for both of you."

Chapter Twenty-nine

On the pretext of arranging for refreshments I left the room and gave directions to Dora that wine and biscuits were to be taken into the library for Mr Ogilvy's guests. Then taking a shawl I walked out through the back of the house and up into the woods.

The ground rose steeply there, behind the house; but I did not slacken my pace. Instead I walked harder, almost running, the breath coming from my body in brief, painful gusts, as if by running I could escape the terrible sadness which was growing up inside me and which I feared might overwhelm me completely. Mr Ogilvy had been to Italy before many times since I had lived at Thirleby Hall; and he had always come back from Italy. But I knew that if he went away this time he would be lost to me for ever; and at that thought I screamed, a long, terrible scream; and I fell to the ground and lay there insensible.

When I opened my eyes at last it was to feel someone's eyes upon me. I knew whose eyes those must be.

She was sitting facing me on a dead log, so still that she herself could have been mistaken for dead wood. In her mouth there was a clay pipe and she had a piece of sacking round her shoulders for warmth. I stared at her and she stared back at me; out here among the trees, the fallen leaves, the tangled grasses, she looked quite different; here she was one with her surroundings, as much a wild creature as a fox or a stoat; and I was no longer conscious of her smell, her filth.

I said, "So I find you here, mother." "Mother"—the word slipped out. But it did not seem to surprise her and after all old women are called "mother" often enough, not only by their sons and daughters. She went on sucking at her pipe and looking at me out of those bright blue eyes.

She said, "And what is the likes of you doing here in the woods?"

"Me?" I repeated in disbelief. "The likes of me?" And then I looked down at my black dress, muddied a little now, but a very proper black dress just the same, especially when it was compared with the sacking rags that she was wearing herself. My disguise, I realized, was complete; to her out here in the woods I appeared as strange and curious a creature as she seemed to be in the kitchens of Thirleby Hall. How could I explain that some part of me felt as much at home in these woods as she did herself? That it was easy for me to imagine myself living out in the wilds, feeding off berries and lichen just as birds do. This part of me, I realized, was well hidden from sight—even from eyes as sharp as hers.

I said, "I often walk here."

"Folks have strange habits," she replied.

Sitting there she looked more like a toad than a woman, I thought. Her skin was tobacco brown and her heavy-lidded eyes would drop shut from time to time, only to snap open again suddenly. I would not have been surprised to see her tongue dart outwards to catch a passing fly.

I had no idea of how long I had been out in the woods. I said, "I must get back." Yet my tongue felt heavy and unwieldy in my mouth and my limbs felt as if they would barely carry me.

She said, "You're tired."

"Yes," I said. "Yes—" and as I spoke my eyes closed and my head dropped forward. More than anything, I realized, I wanted to sleep; I felt so utterly weary, as if all the love and care I had given to Mr Ogilvy in the past few months had left my own spirits quite depleted. And, I thought, if I did sleep, the solution might come to me of what I should do, of how I could prevent Mr Ogilvy from leaving me again. And at last under the indifferent gaze of the old crone I fell asleep.

That sleep was the deepest, the most comforting I have ever known. I drowned in sleep, gorged myself in sleep, refreshed with sleep the furthest recesses of my being. And then as I began to wake I heard sweet sounds of music, trumpets, violins, the tender sounds of woodwind; before my eyes I saw colours more varied and more beautiful than any I had seen in the rainbows which arched over Thirleby Woods, pinks, violets, soft yellows. And then at last I dreamed and in this dream the love I so much craved for, the love I had always longed for, from a child, was mine, it was within my possession. I felt the sense of it warming my heart, causing my heart to swell with joy. And from above there came a voice which told me how much I was loved; and I felt loving arms all round me.

So complete was the sensation of delight that I floated there, like a baby in its cradle, being rocked by an eternal hand; and I did not open my eyes, nor did I feel any desire to open my eyes to see the face of the lover who hovered above me.

I awoke at last. But the dream did not vanish with my awakening; rather the comfort of it remained with me. Smiling I stretched myself feeling altogether restored. Of course I knew the name of my lover; it was Mr Ogilvy.

The log on the other side of the clearing was bare. Once more, as I slept, the old woman had moved on and once again I had failed to put my question to her, to discover what was my name. But in this moment of tranquillity I could regret nothing; now that I was sure of Mr Ogilvy's love, then nothing else was important.

I returned to the Hall to find that Mr Ogilvy had given orders to his valet, to the grooms for a departure the next day.

"He's like that, Mr Ogilvy," remarked Mrs Duckham, spooning with satisfaction the juices over a joint of beef. "That's how gentlemen are. They make their minds up and they're off."

But nothing she said could disturb me. I was sure, I was completely sure that everything would come to my satisfaction. And I had already decided what I should do. It was plain that Mr Ogilvy had never realized his love for me because he saw me always as a housekeeper; I would contrive that he saw me quite differently, and then all would be accomplished. I would surprise him and the surprise would cause the blindfold to fall from his eyes. Certainly I was not as beautiful as Nina Sanctuary had been, but I loved him much more.

I saw no sense in appearing to him in the library in anything but my usual costume. I felt certain that he had to be altogether taken off his guard and I could think of only one way of contriving that this should happen. I would appear to him in his room in the darkness, when everyone was asleep. Then he would recognize my love and our spirits would meet in love as they had already met in my dream.

I waited on him that evening at dinner with special care. He said, "My goodness, Harriet, I shall miss you—" and he leant forward to pat my hand. But I drew back; I could not bear that his hand should touch mine in a gesture of mere affection, or at least not now that I knew that all the passion he could feel was about to be mine. I said, "Yes, sir, thank you, sir," and quietly left the room.

I sat before the mirror for hours, brushing and re-brushing my hair. I remembered the gown of white silk that Nina Sanctuary had worn in her bedroom and I wished that for this occasion that gown could be mine. I could contrive only a plain white shift. And yet as I raised the candle to the glass, I could see my love shining out of my eyes and I felt certain that it could not be withstood.

I waited until the house was quite silent. It was after midnight when I walked down through the house and I knew that everyone would be asleep, including Mr Ogilvy.

The fire in his room was low, but it still threw out a faint light and I saw his dark head against the pillow. I stood for a moment savouring the joy of being in his room, with him; and then I moved forward, the candle in my hand.

I wanted to wake him as gently as I could. One hand was lying on top of the cover; lightly I put my own over it. Although I had scarcely touched him he was disturbed; he turned his head and I heard him speak. What did he say? I bent my head towards him. "Nina," he breathed. "Nina."

He would know a better love than hers. Tenderly, just as I had dreamed of doing, I put my lips to his.

He opened his eyes. Proudly I held up the candle so that he could see my face.

"Harriet?" he said.

"Yes, sir," I replied. "It is Harriet."

"But what—is there something amiss?"

For answer I put down the candle and once more bent forward to embrace him, feeling the cloak of love all round us just as it had been in my dream. For a moment I felt him still beneath my lips. But then he drew back, with a muttered exclamation which I could not understand.

"Sir," I said. "You have not realized—" and I threw my arms round him to convince him of the seriousness of my embrace. But he lifted his hands to my shoulders and shoved me away from him across the room.

"You are mad," he said. "Quite mad."

He was groping for the candle and, finding it, he held it over his head. Behind him on the wall a huge and menacing shadow mounted. "For God's sake," he said, "go back where you belong. Harriet, there is no place for you here."

Chapter Thirty

I LAY on my bed in the room, the same little room that I had once shared with Betsey, the same small bare room. But the wind had come into the room with me, a wind that blustered and tore about the walls, pulling at my hair, swinging me round now this way, now that. And this I endured for several hours, until the very darkest point of the night, when at last the winds fell silent.

Then I was nothing, I was smaller than a baby in its mother's womb. Until hate, or the devil, or the devil's hate, began to rouse me, running into my fingers, my toes, filling my whole body so that I became alive again, fully alive and the devil's child.

By the morning he would be dead. Once before I had wished a death and my wish had been granted. How much stronger now was my wish and how much more certain was I that it would be granted. I paced the room calling on my devil and I felt my heart jumping in my breast and I knew that the devil would do my work. Mr Ogilvy would not see the morning. And at last, triumphant, I fell asleep.

My triumph was short-lived. In my sleep the hatred passed away and grief, the most terrible grief I had ever known, took its place. I was awoken by my own sobbing. He was dead and I had contrived his death. I had killed my father—or the only father I had ever known.

I soaked my face in water from the jug, ice-cold, but my face remained red and swollen. Listlessly, I brushed back my hair, thrust in the pins and prepared to go downstairs. I did not know how to face what lay ahead of me. It only remained now, I thought, to kill myself. Certainly I could not live on with the guilt and remorse which now lay upon my conscience.

I went out onto the upper floor of the house. How huge it was, how empty now that the spirit of the house had departed. What would happen to it now, I wondered? I saw it left empty, crumbling slowly into a ruin.

And behind me a door opened suddenly. "Harriet? Harriet? Where is my breakfast?"

I stood quite still, unable to believe what I had heard. It was only very gradually that I was able to turn round—to see then Mr Ogilvy, a very much alive Mr Ogilvy, an exceedingly disgruntled Mr Ogilvy. "Have you taken leave of your senses?" he demanded. "Altogether? You know I am to be off this morning."

I said, "Yes, sir, at once, sir," and I ran, as fast as I could go, down the stairs and along the passages to the kitchen.

Mrs Duckham was asking too whether I had taken leave of my senses, for I put the kitchen into an uproar. But I arranged before Mr Ogilvy a breakfast like a banquet, a breakfast fit for a prince.

"Hm," he said. And fell to with a good appetite.

When he had satisfied his first hunger, I said, "Sir. I must speak to you."

"Yes?" he said.

"I am very sorry, sir, about . . . "

"Oh that. Say no more, Harriet, you were clearly walking in your sleep."

"But," and then I fell silent. Sleepwalking? Yes of course—why had I not thought of that myself? I must have been sleepwalking, ever since in the wood watched over by the old woman I had fallen asleep. Otherwise, surely I would never have undertaken such a preposterous plan.

But there was something else that I had to ask him, and this was even more difficult. I had to talk to him of Nina Sanctuary, to tell him of the part I had played in her death. But I did not know how I was to do it.

I said, "Sir—" and stopped.

"Yes, Harriet?"

At the kindness in his voice, his smile, the tears came again.

I struggled to hold them back but all I could say was, "I am very sorry, sir, about Miss Nina."

The smile vanished from his face.

"Yes, Harriet."

"I did not mean—" and then my sense of the truth stopped me from going on. Of course I had meant it, I had wished her dead with all my strength. But what had I done? Had wishing her dead been enough? I had wished Mr Ogilvy dead also, and he had not died.

He was looking at me, the expression on his face so weary. He said, as if he had said it to himself many times before, "I called to her to take care. But she would not listen. She would never listen."

"But how ... ?"

"The horse, the horse! A crazed beast. I warned her of that too, but she would insist. I sometimes think ... "

"Yes, sir?"

"That she could not—that she would not have lived long even if the accident had been survived. She was too impatient for life as the rest of us live it, too quick; she was not of this world. The horse had to be shot, I could not let it live on after it had killed her. The most beautiful animal I have ever seen and the least to be trusted."

From the library windows I watched the cavalcade wind its way across the park on the first stage of the journey to Ravello. A coach, several smaller carriages, outriders. I remembered how, all those months ago, he had arrived at Thirleby Hall on horseback, with Nina Sanctuary. Since then she had died and something in Mr Ogilvy had died with her.

And what of me? I had been released, had I not? Nina Sanctuary's death had had a simple explanation after all, in her temperament and that of her favourite mount.

For a moment I had a sensation of freedom as heady as any that I had experienced out riding beside Mr Ogilvy on horseback. Perhaps after all I was not the devil's child, but free to be myself.

And then I remembered the old woman who had sat with me the day before. She was my mother, I was her child. The child of filth.

Chapter Thirty-one

IT WAS a hard winter that year at Swithindale. When I woke each morning it was to find the water frozen in the ewer beside my bed and as I dressed I could see my breath forming shapes in the still cold air of the room. Mr Ogilvy wrote every several weeks from Ravello and his letters spoke of a different world, of breakfasting in the sunshine and of how good the orange crop would be that year. In the bitter cold of a Yorkshire winter I could only shake my head and marvel at such things.

But there was no time for envy; there was too much work to be done. Now, in the place of Mr Ogilvy, I saw the bailiff each morning and went over with him the affairs of the tenants and of the estate. To be sure no important decisions could be mine; but it was I who wrote to Mr Ogilvy about important matters as they arose and I who communicated his replies to the bailiff.

There was also work to be seen to in the house. It had remained unchanged in the years since the death of Nina Sanctuary; now, with Mr Ogilvy's authority to back me, I felt it time to make improvements so that the house would reflect Mr Ogilvy's notable position in the county. Bearing always in mind the decorations I found, I yet ordered new ones to be undertaken, so that when Mr Ogilvy did at last return it would be to a beautiful and welcoming house.

Patrick was still at home at this time assisting his father. He called one day at the Hall. As was proper I received him in the housekeeper's room, where I was busy writing a letter to Mr

Ogilvy. "Sir, with your permission I am undertaking the commission of new drapes for the library . . . "

Patrick, hat and gloves in his hands, sat down in a chair opposite my desk. I thought, as I so often did, that he seemed to bring with him into a room a kind of glow—just as his mother did—of warmth, of love, of spirituality. His eyes were very clear, his expression open. What different creatures we were, I thought, my heart sinking; as we always had been, even in those first days when he and I had played together at the Rectory. In the face of his openness I felt a terrible constraint settling upon me; I did not know what he saw, but I suspected from the pleasure in his smile that what he saw in me he very much liked. But what he would think if he knew the truth, I did not know.

Fearful of what that clear-eyed gaze might discern, I lowered my own to the papers before me and spoke timidly and without ease; until at last he rose, slapping his gloves against his leg, and said that he would bid me good day.

I looked at the empty chair when he had gone and could have wished him back; but I knew that if he did return our conversation would be the same. There was nothing to be done; he and I could speak to each other only over the void of chaos which separated his virtue and my vice, his good and my evil; for so it had been ordained since my birth.

And perhaps Patrick was aware himself of the gulf between us, for it was some time before he came to the Hall again. My next encounter with him was as I was crossing the fields, having been on a visit to one of the outlying farms where a tenant's wife lay ill. He too was on foot and he hailed me from a distance.

As I always did in the open air, I felt less constrained, and watching him cross the ploughed field towards me I felt myself smiling, out of pleasure not so much from the sight of him as from the crisp cold air and the black outline of the hills against the dour winter sky. Yet he may have thought otherwise; for I found his eyes resting on my eager face with delight and surprise.

"I was about to visit you, Harriet," he said.

"And you would have found me not at home."

"So I see."

We turned to walk in the direction of the Hall and as always the sight of the great mansion filled me with pleasure. I stopped and Patrick stopped beside me. "It is a fine house," I said.

"Indeed," he replied. "You are a member of a fine household."

That was not what I had meant at all; it was not as a member of the household that I had gazed upon the house, for now that Mr Ogilvy was away and I had been left in charge, I regarded myself in my fancy as mistress of the Hall. I looked up at Patrick, almost to contradict him; and then reality returned to me. But not in desolation; for I had still my expectations.

"Mr Ogilvy is a good employer," I said.

"And what news is there of Mr Ogilvy?" he asked. "Is he well?"

I nodded. "He is very well—in fact, I am sure he is much better. When he returns he will be quite recovered."

"From his mourning?"

"It will all be forgotten."

"And what of you, Harriet? What of yourself? My mother asks me often to bring you to Swithindale—she says that she so rarely sees you."

"I have so much to do," I said, and spread out my hands in a gesture which included both the house and the large estate through which we walked.

"Indeed, but you also have much freedom. I think you should enjoy it. As a matter of fact—" and emphatically he smacked his gloved hands together, "I believe you should come to Swithindale for Christmas dinner."

"But my duties at the Hall . . . "

"Will all be finished by the evening, just as my father's duties will be over. We shall have a family supper, Maria will be there. Harriet, you must come, I insist."

His face was alight with pleasure. So, I thought, my heart dull, Mr Ogilvy had looked at Nina Sanctuary, but never at me.

"Thank you, Patrick," I said at last. "I will see if it can be arranged."

In fact, there was no reason why I should not go to the Rectory on Christmas night—except for my own reluctance to do so. Patrick's invitation was followed by one from his mother, urging me most warmly to accept their hospitality, suggesting even that I might spend the whole day at Swithindale, attending morning church with them. This I could not do; but I agreed at last to allow myself to be transported into Swithindale during the afternoon.

Christmas Day itself was dark and even as the trap took me into Swithindale in time to join the evening festivities the light was fading. The air was very cold and I was glad of the warmer at my feet. How great then, and how enjoyable, was the contrast with the parlour of the Rectory, where there was a hearty fire burning and seven or eight friendly faces to greet me.

It had indeed been a long time since my last visit and the children were so much grown that I could scarcely fit names to all of them. Maria was of course the same, only gentler even than I remembered her and quieter. But the warmth of her smile and of her handclasp had not changed.

I had come grudgingly, with little anticipation of pleasure, ready to impress upon my old teacher and my old companions at school that though I might be a servant I was one of the grandest kind, bearing responsibilities which were very considerable. Now all that was forgotten. I found myself simply delighted to be in their company again.

We sat, all of us, at a great round table. It had been spread with a sparkling white cloth and decorated, as Charlotte on my one hand, and Maria on the other pointed out to me, by the younger girls. At the centre of the table there was a fine épergne, worthy to be compared with the best pieces of table silver at the Hall; and around it were little dishes of filigree silver, filled with sweetmeats made by Maria.

And yet it was not the splendour of the table which most impressed me, nor the delicacy of the dishes that were spread before me. I had seen many parties at the Hall, particularly in the course of Nina Sanctuary's stay there, which had been far more glittering and splendid occasions. But what I had not found elsewhere was the love and friendship which this family extended to me.

I looked all round the table; from the Reverend Ponsonby himself, his face red, his white hair standing up like a crown, to my dear Mrs Ponsonby, appearing older and more fatigued than she had done in my days as her pupil, but still to my eye beautiful. And as I observed and rejoiced, so I found Patrick smiling at me across the table and raising his glass to me in a salute.

When supper was finished and the dishes cleared away, then there was an entertainment. Maria played the piano, Patrick sang some ballads and the younger children recited. I sat beside Mrs Ponsonby, clapping all the items most vigorously and wishing that I could join in; but learning to play an instrument or to sing had not been part of my education.

When the time came at last for me to leave, Mrs Ponsonby

embraced me closely. "I feel you have come back to us, Harriet," she said. "You are one of us again."

She spoke with her arms round me in farewell; and I felt myself instantly drawing back. For she had reminded me of what in the course of the evening I had forgotten. Nothing had changed; I had not returned to them. They were and always would be creatures of heaven and I was my mother's child.

Chapter Thirty-two

THROUGHOUT THE winter Patrick continued to visit me. We walked, we talked and he brought me books to read and sometimes a little bunch of flowers, or some of his mother's oatcake. As well as oatcake his mother often sent loving messages which I would receive always with pleasure, and at the same time the certainty that if Mrs Ponsonby knew all that there was to know of myself, then she would not love me as she claimed. When invitations came for me to visit the Rectory, I pretended always to be too much occupied; and too, I insisted that I could make no formal arrangement with Patrick; only that if he did come I would see if my duties permitted me to take the time to walk with him or, if the weather was too bad, then we would sometimes sit together in the library.

The house by now was in thoroughly good order, grumble as Mrs Duckham did about my "interference." It had had to be made ready, I felt, though for what I did not clearly admit to myself. Every corner of the house had been thoroughly turned out, preserves had been made and counted, hams salted, beer brewed. There was nothing in the house that I did not know of and which I felt was in anything but perfect order. Once we received news of Mr Ogilvy's return, it would be the work of only a couple of days to remove the dustcovers and set the house asparkle.

In February Mrs Minim died and was duly buried. The maids and Mrs Duckham wept of course, as they expected themselves to do; I scarcely expected to feel grief and was surprised, in the event, to find it. She had lived an honest life, I thought to myself, and had not in the end done badly by any of us. I wrote to Mr Ogilvy. "Sir, you will be grieved to hear . . . " I arranged for her possessions to be packed up and dispatched to her only living relative, that I knew of; a sister at Wakefield.

As the spring came I found myself growing daily more impatient for news of Mr Ogilvy's return. When he left he had said nothing of the date of his return; but I had understood, I had most clearly understood, that he was going for the winter, to avoid the rigours of another Yorkshire December; and that once the year had turned, then he would give his thoughts to coming back to Thirleby Hall.

But March gave way to April, April to May, and still the expected message did not come. His letters, increasingly cheerful, spoke of the great content he had found there in his village in Southern Italy and it began to seem as if he might not return before high summer.

I spoke increasingly to Patrick of my concern.

"Ah," he said, a look of reminiscence on his face, "that coast is very beautiful. I am not surprised that Mr Ogilvy lingers there."

And I would ask him to describe it to me again, or as much of it as he could remember.

One afternoon in May he came to see me bearing a great bunch of bluebells in his hands.

"They are the very first, Harriet," he said, "from the little clump of beech trees up in the wood. But I am sorry—" and he looked down at them, wry-faced, "they are already wilting."

They were indeed, the heads were bowed and drooping. But the scent was still there, and as it always did, that scent brought tears to my eyes, for no reason that I knew.

"My dear Harriet, please Harriet," said Patrick, himself in great distress. "Let me throw the wretched things away at once—"

I did my best to smile through my tears. "No, please," I said. "Of all wild flowers these are the ones I love the best. That is why I am crying."

In his pleading he had put a hand on my arm. I looked down at that hand now, the fair skin, the short golden hairs glinting on the back of it. And he looked down at his hand too and said, "Harriet, you must know . . . "

A terrible fear came over me then at the thought of what he

might say. I said, "Come, Patrick, we must find water for the flowers."

"Harriet," he said again; but, the flowers in my hands, I had whisked myself away.

Sitting that evening before my solitary supper, I remembered the incident and felt again that same fear. How could Patrick expect me to love him, I wondered; could he not see that all my love had been given long ago to Mr Ogilvy?

Chapter Thirty-three

THE DAY I had been waiting for so long arrived at last. In July, when the whole valley lay beaming in golden sunlight, Mr Ogilvy returned home. I could have wished for no better day for his return.

To welcome him I summoned all the servants to the front hall and stood myself at the head of the line. The great front doors were thrown back, as I had seldom seen them in all my years at the Hall; I watched the procession coming towards us across the park and my excitement could hardly be contained.

The leading carriage came to a halt and one of the footmen went forward to open the door. I saw a head leaning forward and I prepared for my first sight for so many months of the thick, dark hair, the smile of kindness.

And Mr Ogilvy got down from the carriage. Of course Mr Ogilvy got down from the carriage; but my smile of joyful welcome became instantly a look of startled amazement. I could scarcely believe that this was indeed Mr Ogilvy, whom I had loved for most of my life; it was rather an old man, somewhat bent, his hair grizzled. Far from restoring him to health, his stay in Italy seemed to have aged him more than I would have thought possible. In any other place I might not have known him.

But I, it was clear, had not changed. "Harriet," he said; and stretching out his hand he walked towards me with a smile of pleasure on his face, that same smile that I remembered so well. I was able to compose myself. "Sir," I said, curtseying low, "welcome home."

"Thank you, Harriet," he said. "I am exceedingly glad to have arrived. What a journey." And then he turned to the line of servants, nodding and smiling to each one.

I found my thoughts to be in a turmoil of confusion. I was twenty-two years old; the man to whom I had given almost every waking thought for so long was fifty-five—sixty even. Old enough, certainly, to be my father. I loved him still, and I did not doubt for a moment that I loved him. But not, I realized now, as a wife might love her husband, rather as a daughter would look up to and respect her father. All my plans had gone toward engineering for myself a place at Mr Ogilvy's side and now, even if there should be such a place, I knew I would not want it.

Mr Ogilvy was much occupied on the days after his return with the work of the estate. There I thought I had done well for him, but there had been many decisions which had had to be left for his instruction; so that he was shut away with the bailiff, going over the accounts, discussing the various yields. Now I found myself truly a housekeeper and nothing else and fretting within the strict bounds which this life set up for me.

I decided, and the decision came to me like a clap of thunder, that I must leave Thirleby Hall. Mr Ogilvy's absence might not have accomplished for him a return to perfect health but something certainly had been accomplished for me in his absence. I was a young woman now and a strong and competent one, ready to move away from this world of Thirleby Hall which had contained me all my life.

But before I was able thoroughly to examine my new idea and find out all its implications, another event occurred.

Mr Ogilvy had been back at Thirleby Hall for a week. The household was running smoothly as ever and everything was well, except that I was bored. But beneath my boredom there ran a current of excitement; for I felt sure that changes now were bound to come.

I was on my way to the library to see Mr Ogilvy one afternoon when I met one of the housemaids on the stairs. "Is the master alone?" I asked.

"No, m'm, please m'm," bobbed the silly creature. "The Reverend Ponsonby is with him and Mr Patrick as well."

"Ah." I stood considering for a moment and then decided to return to my room until the visitors had left. But before I could do so, Mr Ogilvy came to the door of the library and called out to me. "Harriet, come here, would you?"

I hastened forward, obedient as always to his bidding, and without a thought of whom I should find there, went briskly into the room. Patrick and his father were standing by the window looking out over the park; and I realized then that I had not seen Patrick since Mr Ogilvy's return. He turned now and smiled at me; in that moment of his smile I remembered the first time I had seen him, as a child, and the first time we had encountered each other when he had grown into a young man; I thought as I had done then that his smile was the most loving that I had ever seen and I thought too that I could wish no greater happiness than to live within the blessing of that smile for the rest of my life.

I stood silent in the moment of my awareness. I could feel warmth spreading throughout my body from the warmth I felt within my heart. It had been a long winter, a cold winter, but I felt sure now that the winter was over.

And then I felt my hand go to that scar on my arm, the scar of my pact with the devil. How could I have thought even for a moment that Patrick and I . . . ? We were creatures from different worlds, as surely as if after our deaths we had taken our due places, his in heaven, mine in hell.

"Well now, Harriet," said Mr Ogilvy. Behind me, he had clearly realized nothing of what had taken place, although Patrick, I felt sure, was aware of the movement of expressions over my face. I saw again the look of intense concern which he had shown when I had cried before him. He had felt me turn away from him that moment.

"Well now, Harriet," said Mr Ogilvy again, jovially. "We have news for you. Patrick here is to have his living at last."

Formally I congratulated Patrick.

He was smiling towards Mr Ogilvy. "I have my excellent patron to thank," he said.

"It is nearby?" I asked.

"No, we have had to give up hope of that. But Mr Ogilvy has been good enough to give my name to friends on the other side of the county."

"So you will be going away?"

"I am afraid, Harriet," he said, "that I must."

Mr Ogilvy and the Reverend Ponsonby had drawn a little away from us by this time. Patrick glanced round at them and seeing them deep in their own conversation said to me, hesitating just a little, "Harriet, there is something—if you wished, you could come with me."

I drew back. "As your housekeeper?"

"Housekeeper? Heavens, no." He laughed. "Dear Harriet, I express myself so badly, you must have patience with me. Not as my housekeeper, but as my wife."

It was a moment of joy and pain almost not to be borne. He had asked me to be his wife, in the moment of my realizing both that I loved him dearly and that, different as we were, no relationship of a lasting kind was possible for us.

And indeed I could not bear that moment. "No, no," I said and turning, tears starting from my eyes, I fled from the room.

I resolved that there would be an end of it. Even before Patrick left for his new and distant living there would be no more walks together in the woods or out across the fields. Instead I would turn my mind to my other plans for leaving Thirleby Hall and seeking to make my way in the world outside. And now I knew that I must indeed leave, for to stay on at Thirleby Hall, without the precious companionship which Patrick offered me, would be sadness indeed.

Once again I was summoned to the library. Mr Ogilvy had eaten a good dinner and was sitting at his ease. For once it was too hot even in that stately room for a fire to be needed; the lights had not been lit and the room lay in the pale light of dusk. I entered quietly and greeted Mr Ogilvy in a more subdued fashion than usual, standing with my hands clasped in front of me.

"Well, Harriet," he said. "I hear you have been busy in my absence."

"Oh yes, sir," I began. "The house has been cleaned . . . "

"I am sure it has," he interrupted. "But my statement referred to a more personal matter than the cleaning of my house. Young Patrick—his father tells me that he is deep in love and means to marry you."

Hearing those words I could not prevent a tremor of feeling in my heart. But "Yes, sir," I said calmly, my eyes still turned downwards.

"So," he said. "I must seek a new housekeeper."

"Yes, sir," I said. "I think you must. But I will not marry Patrick Ponsonby."

"What? You will not?"

"I should say I cannot."

"But Harriet, really, I must protest. It is an excellent match, it is a far better match . . . "

"Yes, sir," I said again, in my deliberately wooden tones. "It is much too good a match. I have not forgotten who I am."

"Who you are? You are a young woman of excellent character to whom I have with trust been able to leave the running of my affairs for a six month or more."

"Thank you sir. I meant—by birth. It is my birth that is in question."

"Ah," he nodded. "When you came here to Thirleby Hall you were too young to be told the story and since then . . . "

"My mother was a beggar woman, sir," I said. "I have seen her for myself and I know that my birth was of the very lowest."

"You have seen her?" He looked startled. "But no, Harriet, that is impossible."

"I have, I have," I insisted. And now the tears began to flow down my cheeks. "She was a beggar woman of the lowest kind, she came here to Thirleby Hall, I knew her at once."

"Harriet, calm yourself." He took me by the arm and led me to a chair. "Here," and he poured out a little wine into a glass and gave it to me. "Drink and sit with me for a moment. I see I have been gravely wrong in not speaking to you of this before."

The wine felt harsh against my tongue in that first moment but then I found it wonderfully soothing. I drank again from the glass, conscious all the time of his look of concern.

"Now, Harriet," he said at last. "It is in truth quite impossible that you should have seen your mother since you were a very small child. I saw your mother dead at Steepleton Fair before ever you came here."

"Dead?"

He nodded. "Yes, poor woman. She died there at the Fair and rather than have you sent to the poorhouse I brought you back to live here under my protection."

"But how did she die? Who was she?"

"I know very little. No one there knew who she was. She was travelling alone except for you. She was without means. She died beside you, as you slept. At the inn they did not know what to do with you and so I brought you here where at least there was food enough for you. And shelter."

"But—who was the beggar woman who came to the Hall?"

"Harriet, there are so many. It was to save you from such a fate, living and dying out there in the open, that I brought you here. I hope you have been content."

"Content?" I looked back over my life, as over a black shroud, relieved only here and there by threads of gold. But it had been a life; I don't know that it could have been any different. "Mr Ogilvy," I said. "Is that all you know of my mother?"

He looked at me. "I think, Harriet," he said at last, "that she was a good woman who had fallen upon hard times, as only too many do in these difficult days that we live in. They thought at the inn where I found you that she had died of starvation; but you, although dirty in your dress, did not starve. You should not think ill of your mother, Harriet. She was travelling on foot, and had been doing so for a long time, with what goal in mind I do not know. And in the end the journey was too much for her. But she must have cared for you—she gave you her own bread."

"Then I was not a tinker child?"

"Your mother was not a tinker. I wish I could tell you more of who she was. But your birth, Harriet, was not—" again he hesitated, "could not have been as disreputable as you thought. I did not know that you had imagined such things."

"I was told in the kitchen—"

"They knew nothing in the kitchen. I am only sorry I did not speak of this to you before." He stood up and came to put his hands on my shoulders, looking down at me protectively. "Now, Harriet, enough of the past. Let us think of the future; for you there lies ahead a future as bright as you deserve. I cannot commend young Ponsonby highly enough."

But the cold waters of panic were rising again all round me. I stepped back from Mr Ogilvy's embrace, my lips stiff, my heart like stone. "It makes no difference, sir," I said. "I cannot marry him. And I will not."

He looked into my face. But there I made sure he would find no clue as to my reasons.

He sighed. "I feel sure, Harriet, that there is something that you do not understand."

"Sir," I said, and now I began to be angry. "There are things that *you* do not understand."

"Perhaps, perhaps. But this is foolishness, Harriet. At least reflect—do not give an answer at once. Is it perhaps his religion? But you have always attended church regularly."

"I cannot say. I cannot marry him," I repeated.

"Very well. I will press you no more. But I think that the young man himself will not give up so easily. His feeling for you seems very deep—" and again he sighed, and passed a tired hand over his face. I thought how old he had become in Italy, or how much my view of him had changed in the months of his absence. It was hard indeed to see this man as the passionate lover of Nina Sanctuary.

And yet I would always love him.

"Goodnight, sir," I said. "You must not concern yourself—"

"About you?" He laughed. "How could I not? You and I, Harriet, have been together for a long time."

Chapter Thirty-four

I LAY awake for many hours that night, reflecting on what Mr Ogilvy had told me. So my mother had not been the filthy old beggar woman who had called for scraps at our own kitchen door; she had been instead an ordinary woman, the wife of a labourer, or an artisan perhaps who had fallen on hard times and who had denied herself food to let me live. How much I wished that I could bring her face into my memory.

That I could not do however hard I tried. And yet as I thought back, my eyes open in the darkness, although I could not bring her face to mind, I could feel a kind hand and I could hear a soft voice. No indeed, Mr Ogilvy had been right, my mother had not been a tinker woman; rather she had been a quiet, gentle person who had suffered very much and some of her suffering, at least, had been endured on my behalf.

And now all the more I regretted my own wickedness—my hatred of Nina Sanctuary, my anger against the world. My mother had loved me and would have brought me up a gentle child; but finding myself alone I had been able to do nothing better than to ally myself with the devil.

I sat up in bed, lit my candle and looked at the mark on my arm. It was still there, plainly to be seen, white against the brown. I knew now that I would have it for ever.

Mr Ogilvy had told me of Patrick's determination and the next morning I saw it for myself. He presented himself before me looking as he always did, bright, cheerful, only now with a little anxiety to dull the blue of his eyes. I received him with civility only.

"I think, Harriet," he said, "that you may be anxious about my family. But my mother herself has asked me to say that you would be most welcome among us."

I had not expected this, and for a moment I felt tears at the back of my eyes. How I longed to accept this kindness, but the more he offered me kindness the more I knew that I could not accept it. Had he approached me with bad temper, with oaths, then I might have felt that the place he offered was an appropriate one for me. But the more he smiled, his voice low with feeling, the more I felt that at all costs I must not agree to take what he offered me, for to do so would be to ruin his life. My own life was already sullied; I had sullied it myself all those years ago when I had been scarcely more than a child.

He realized at last that I was adamant. "Very well then Harriet," he said, his face shadowed. "I understand that in some way I must be unacceptable to you. I wish you could explain to me why. But I hope at least that you will remain on terms of friendship with my mother and my sisters; we all love you very dearly."

When the door had closed behind him, I put my head down on my desk and sobbed till I thought my heart would break. There was nothing to be done. Nothing at all to be done.

Patrick was to leave Swithindale to take up his new living in only a few weeks' time. As the date of his going drew nearer, I felt more and more that I must go myself; but further away, to London perhaps, to the south. I was willing even to contemplate going abroad. England itself seemed too small to hold us both, the danger was too great.

"I think, Harriet," said Mr Ogilvy, "that you should do nothing in haste. I do not understand your impatience. If you will only wait, I am sure a fine position can be found for you—though perhaps not as good a one as you have here. You are so young still."

"I have made up my mind," I said.

"Amazing," he murmured, looking at me. "Such firmness, such obstinacy in a young girl. Well, I see, Harriet, that we must do what we can. But I can promise nothing before the spring—besides, what should I do here without you?"

So I would live through another winter at the Hall, and this time a winter which would not be relieved by Patrick's friendship. I would have instead the companionship of Mr Ogilvy, we would no doubt renew our old habit of chatting beside the library fire, talking of books, or travel, just as I had done with Patrick. But it would not be the same. I was used now to a different life.

On the day before his departure was to take place Patrick came to the Hall to say goodbye to Mr Ogilvy and to me. Mr Ogilvy called me into the library and Patrick and I said farewell to each other under his benevolent eye. He said, "Of course, I shall be back often—" but his voice was quiet, without hope. He said it, I thought, to comfort himself rather than to console me; for I would give no sign that I needed consolation.

Nor that day did I think I wanted it. I had cried for Patrick's lost brightness and I had not cried again. I was no Daedalus—I knew that the sun was too bright for me and that I could survive only close to the earth, my mother. I kept my eyes to the ground like a mole, seeking the dark, substantial comfort of food, drink and shelter and leaving my other wants unrecognized. I was conscious of the ironclad walls around me and of the hollowness within and allowed myself to feel nothing else.

I went about my duties that day with a swift efficiency which caused many a grumble amongst the maids. "What's got into her, then, Mrs Duckham?" I heard a plaintive voice say in the kitchen, after I had ordered the pots scrubbed out a second time. At first I ignored it; but then I thought that someone who did not work was not worthy of a place at Thirleby Hall, certainly not of the good food and shelter that the Hall provided for all its members. I turned to confront the complaining woman. "There's food here for those who work," I instructed her. "And for no one else." And I left her startled face behind me.

That evening I shut up all the doors and windows of the Hall with greater vigour than usual, sliding the bolts to on the great front doors, making sure all the windows were firmly closed. Then, my lamp in my hand, just as once Mrs Minim had walked with the lamp in hers, I walked the corridors of the Hall.

How still it was, I thought, how quiet. Before the library fire, his dogs at his feet, Mr Ogilvy dozed; the maids had gone early to bed. I raised the lamp above my head to catch in its pale glow the sculpted heads, the painted faces which lined the walls, the corridors, and I rested my hand with affection upon the stone pate of Julius Caesar. All was quiet, all was still, all was ordered. My kingdom was complete; the invaders had been repulsed.

But my contentment lasted barely a moment. I held it still there in my hand for a few seconds only. And then as if before a gale, an overwhelming blizzard, the walls of my being swayed and fell. What was my safety, what was any of it, if Patrick had gone? I almost fainted; and, my head swimming, I took with difficulty my last few steps to the housekeeper's room.

I closed the door and stood leaning against it. Except for the lamp in my hand the room was dark; but in any case my eyes were closed as I struggled to recover from the tumult of emotion I felt blowing all about me. And then I heard a voice coming gently out of the darkness. "Harriet? Is it you, Harriet?"

I opened my eyes, I held the lamp above my head; and there standing before me was Patrick himself.

I do not remember moving towards him or that he moved towards me. I only know that we found ourselves in the middle of the room, the lamp set safely down, and that his arms were round me and mine around him; and I knew that never again would I feel lonely or unloved.

Our bodies fitted together as into one mould; and feeling his body so hard against my own soft flesh, I could remember again that day in the woods when I had witnessed the embrace of Mr Ogilvy and Nina Sanctuary. I knew now that what I had thought that day to be impossible had in fact come true; I had found someone who loved me as much as Nina Sanctuary had been loved and I loved him in return. This was the love I had always dreamt of.

But although now our love for each other was plain, I had to explain to Patrick why I had so firmly refused him; and feeling him so close and dear within my arms I felt for the first time that I could explain it all to him and that he would understand and help me to find forgiveness.

I could hardly bear to move away from him and for many moments indeed I did not; but then we sat together before the fire, my hand in his, and falteringly I told him my story.

I omitted nothing; I told him all I could remember of my life at Thirleby Hall, of my arrival there, of my first unceremonious washing under the pump, of the contempt which the other servants expressed for me, a foundling child. And I found it easier to tell than I had imagined; for not once did he reproach me, priest though he was, for the wicked temper that I had shown, for my anger; instead he pressed my hand soothingly and put his lips to my cheek in consolation.

I told him everything. I told him of the rat's bite and made his fingers trace the scar on my arm. I told him of the beating Nina Sanctuary had given me and of my determination to have my revenge upon her; I told him even of my love for Mr Ogilvy and of my desperate attempt to persuade him of it. And at the end of my recital he held me within his arms and rocked me like a child.

I waited then for what he would say. Already I could feel my heart hardening; now, I felt sure, he would tell me that, wicked as I was, I could not be his bride and that we must part for ever. And I prepared myself to hear his harsh words and to accept them, for I knew that I deserved them all.

But he said not one harsh word. Instead he turned my face to his and said, "Harriet, to me you are all the world. We shall be so very happy."

Now I struggled free, my face incredulous. "But," I said, "you cannot mean it."

"Indeed I do," he said. "Just as I believe in forgiveness and in atonement. Harriet, no doubt you have had wicked thoughts in your heart, but you have also suffered a very great deal at the hands of others. Surely now you have atoned for all the evil that was within you. Do you not feel this yourself?"

I felt indeed, leaning my head against his shoulder, a great sense of comfort and of restoration. "Yes, yes," I found myself murmuring.

And yet for me then the absolution he had given me thus in love was not quite enough. I had carried this burden of sin and guilt within me for so many years that it was hard to relinquish it in a moment. How often I had referred myself to the devil my mentor. How could I be sure that the devil now had departed from me?

Haltingly, as best I could, I explained this to Patrick. Again he listened, his face gentle and concerned. How had I ever earned such love, such kindness, I wondered? And I knew that I had not earned it, but that it had come to me by the grace of God; and now I began to accept that the devil my mentor had at last begun to leave me.

Patrick pondered on what I had told him. "I think, Harriet," he said at last, "we should go to my father. He will know what to do. I think we must ask him for his blessing."

I shrank back. "No," I said. "No—how can I tell your father

what I have told you?"

He pressed my hand warmly in both of his. "Harriet, you are no longer alone—you must know that now. I will talk to my father of your fears and there will not be the slightest need to tell him everything that you have told me, if you do not wish it. Now, Harriet, you must trust me."

And then indeed I began to trust him. As I had once trusted my mother, as latterly I had trusted Mr Ogilvy. And I found within myself that wealth of trust and love which had remained shut away for so many years that I had forgotten its existence.

Chapter Thirty-five

ONCE MORE Harry drove me in the trap to Swithindale. It was hard to mount the step, it was hard to remain sitting as if at my ease, for I was truly afraid; the devil within me fought hard to retain the last part of me that he possessed.

Harry set me down by the green, as he always had done; I walked past the little houses, past the shops, past the dressmaker's establishment. There, in the distance, stood the grey, square Rectory, and beside it the squat Norman tower of the church. Hardest of all it was to walk the path from the lych gate to the church door; then, truly, did the devil within me fight. How he sneered! "You think you are worthy of love, you who lived to be bitten by rats, chastised by your betters?"

My step grew slower and at last I stopped altogether, leaning for some support against a funeral monument. I looked up—into the face of a stone angel. There in the carved eyes I found the forgiveness that I had seen on Patrick's face.

And so the strength came to me to walk on, into the church where Patrick was waiting for me.

We knelt together before the altar, not touching but closely side by side. In full regalia the Reverend Ponsonby came from the vestry and held up his hand in blessing over us. I felt through him the strength and power of God's kingdom.

I was still Harriet Dark; and at times I knew the devil would return to me to whisper words of pride and vainglory. But I knew too that though anger, vanity and wickedness might be in my heart, I was nonetheless a child of God. On my side there was a greater power than the power of evil; to triumph over evil I had only to invoke the power of love.